He loved the girl and wanted to marry her, but how could he possibly fulfil her aunt's challenge?

"You have a glib tongue, young man," the countess said. "Now my challenge for you to win dear Annise's favor is this…"

Eduard leaned forward with anticipation.

"…both of her parents, the Count and Countess de Brisson have been seized by the revolutionists and are in a prison. We do not know where. Your assignment is to get them out of prison. Once they are safe, I will give you my blessings to marry the young lady."

Eduard leaned back, feeling the blood drain from his face. He could not speak. Finally, after a long minute, he stammered, "H—How do you expect me to do that?"

During the Reign of Terror in France in the late 1700s, the common people amused themselves by watching the heads of the nobility roll, severed by the guillotine. When Eduard Saulnier falls in love with Countess Annise de Brisson in 1793, he fears that, as a commoner, he will never be allowed to court her. But Annise is staying with her aunt because her parents have been sized by the revolutionaries and condemned to die by the guillotine. Eduard approaches the old lady for permission to court Annise, knowing his chances are slim. However, he is totally unprepared for the old countess's answer—yes, he may court and marry Annise, *after* he gets her parents out of prison…any way he can.

KUDOS for *Love's Dangerous Challenge*

In *Love's Dangerous Challenge* by Ellynore Seybold, Annise de Brisson is a young French countess. In January 1793, the French revolutionaries storm their chateau and arrest her parents, but Annise's father and mother order her to flee, and she escapes, making her way to her aunt's. There, she meets Eduard Saulnier, who falls instantly in love with her. When Eduard asks her aunt for permission to court her, the aunt agrees on one condition. He must first rescue her parents by any means necessary. Distraught at the impossible task that has been set before him, Eduard begins a harrowing journey that will change many lives forever. While this is a story of young love, it is much more than a romance. It's a history lesson about a turbulent time in the world's past, with characters that seem so real you feel like you know them and vivid descriptions that make you feel you are right there with them. A great read. ~ *Taylor Jones, The Review Team of Taylor Jones & Regan Murphy*

Love's Dangerous Challenge is the story of the French revolution in 1793. Seventeen-year-old Annise de Brisson lives with her parents in their chateau outside of Paris. One day in early January, the revolutionaries raid the estate and arrest her parents, along with stealing almost everything of value. Her parents order Annise to flee and she runs to a servant's. He hides her and then takes her to her aunt's chateau where she finds safety. Because the new regime wants her parents' land, they are to go on trial for high treason, even though they have done nothing wrong. Annise is desperate to save her parents, so she appeals to some influential men who come to a party at her aunt's house. She does not succeed in getting her parents released, but the men do take pity on her and have her parents moved from the prison they are in to the tower where the royal family has been imprisoned. At this same party, Annise meets Eduard Saulneir, who is immediately smitten. Her aunt tells him he is free to court her niece, just as soon as he gets her parents released from prison. Seybold's character development is superb, her characters both realistic and enchanting. Though the story is a basically romance, the author manages to convey both the traumatic and terrifying situations these people find themselves in as well as the courage and determination the survivors had to show in order to survive, giving us a glimpse into history that we don't usually see. Very well done. ~ *Regan Murphy, The Review Team of Taylor Jones & Regan Murphy*

Love's

Dangerous
Challenge

Ellynore Seybold

A Black Opal Books Publication

GENRE: HISTORICAL ROMANCE/ROMANTIC SUSPENSE

This is a work of fiction. Names, places, characters and incidents are either the product of the author's imagination or are used fictitiously, and any resemblance to any actual persons, living or dead, businesses, organizations, events or locales is entirely coincidental. All trademarks, service marks, registered trademarks, and registered service marks are the property of their respective owners and are used herein for identification purposes only. The publisher does not have any control over or assume any responsibility for author or third-party websites or their contents.

DEDICATION

To all lovers of history

Chapter 1

Early January, an estate outside of Paris, France:

Annise awoke from a deep sleep, hearing shouting and banging. She jumped out of bed, threw a wool robe over her cotton nightgown, and went to the window. She looked down at a mob of people dressed in ragged clothes, armed with edged tools, screaming, and shouting. The sound of metal hitting the heavy oak front door reverberated throughout the house. Quickly, she put on the peasant clothes she liked to wear for every day. She rushed down the flight of stairs and reached the foyer where her mother stood next to her father sitting in a wheeled chair. Two young footmen, dressed in fancy uniform, tried desperately to hold the double door in place by holding a heavy console table with a marble top against it.

"Mama, Papa, what is happening?" Annise shouted, feeling the blood drain from her face.

"The revolutionaries are raiding our chateau," her mother, Azelma, said, trying to remain calm. "Save yourself. Wear the gray cloak and run to Yves's house and—"

Before Azelma could finish the sentence, the heavy door gave way. The console table was toppled over breaking the marble. Men, carrying axes, pikes, and sickles rushed in. The two footmen were the first thing that caught their attention. Annise stood petrified next to her parents, Count and Countess de Brisson, watching the men in ragged clothes surround the footmen. She heard the cries of pain. They soon ended with two bloody heads raised on a pike above the mob.

Both women gasped and screamed.

"Courage," Count Peter said, slightly above a whisper. "Save yourselves, both of you. If it wasn't for my broken leg, I too would flee out back to Yves's house."

The mother and seventeen-year-old-daughter just stood there, ashen faced and silent. Meanwhile, the men cleared the doorway as more people poured in. They looked with awe at the black and white marble tile floor and the crystal chandeliers with burning whale-wax candles. They stood in front of the large mirrors on two walls that reflected back the light and gave the foyer an endless look.

"You stay where you are," commanded a middle-aged man in coarse peasant clothes. "Where is the rest of your family?"

"This is all of us," Count Peter de Brisson said.

"You lie," said the man, slapping him in the face.

"No," Azelma said, "He does not lie. We are a small family."

The man gave the countess a cold look, but did not dare to strike her. "You people just stay where you are."

The men and women went running through the chateau like dogs left out of a cage after a long confinement.

"Azelma, Annise, you two sneak out when you see your chance."

"Peter, I'm your wife. I will not abandon you. I love you, and I will stay with you." Turning to her daughter, she whispered, "Annise, watch for the first chance you get to escape. Remember to wear the gray cloak that is hidden near the back door. Very important."

"Where shall I go? How will you find me?" Annise sobbed with tears running down her cheeks.

"Annise, stop being a baby," the count said in a stern whisper. "This is a time you need to show your Brisson courage. Remember what plans we had made should this situation ever arise. Now show the valor I know is in you."

"Yes, Father, I remember," she said, leaning over and hugging him while whispering into his ear, "I'll seek refuge at Yves's house and have him help me get to Aunt Melina's. She will shelter me until we can all get back together."

"*That* is my dear daughter," he said, stroking her blonde hair.

At the top of the graceful staircase, a group of women were laughing and shouting, "Make way for the queen."

One woman, dressed in Azelma's royal blue ball-gown and carrying a large silk fan, slowly descended the stairs, accompanied by other women, wearing an assortment of the countesses dresses.

The "queen" slowly walked up to the three Brisson's and closed the fan with a loud whop.

"Off with their heads," she shouted.

Azelma and Annise recoiled in horror. At the same time, some men rushed into the foyer carrying a wicker basket, full of wine bottles. They pulled the corks and passed out the bottles to the delight and cheers of everyone.

"Go, Annise, save yourself while they are distracted," Azelma whispered.

"Come too, Mama."

"No, I stay with my husband, no matter what. Now just casually make your way out back."

The foyer's light was diminishing, as the wind

coming in the open doorway extinguished the candles. Annise picked up an empty wine bottle from the floor and slowly walked along, pretending to be drinking. By the dim light, and dressed like a peasant, she blended in with the scene, as she made her way to the back door of the small palace. In a trunk used for her father's gardening clothes, she retrieved the gray wool cloak her mother had emphasized she must take. She wrapped the heavy cloak around herself and went out the back door. There were many footprints in the light snow. All the servants had fled. She followed the footprints until she could see the farmhouse, Yves and his family lived in. There were no footprints leading to his house. Annise circled a long way around the house, approaching from the back. To her relief there was no snow near the house, due to the shelter of the grape arbor. She banged on the door as hard as she could.

It seemed forever before she heard a grumpy voice, "I'm coming, I'm coming. Who is it?"

Annise remained silent. She feared that someone might have stepped out of the chateau and might hear her. To her relief, she heard the door being unlocked and opened a crack.

"Oh, it's you, Mademoiselle Annise. What is the problem?"

"There is a mob raiding the chateau. Mama told me to come here and hide."

"Come in, come in, child," he said, while opening

wide enough for her to slip in. "You are shaking. Let me wake my wife to take care of you."

"No, don't wake madame. Now that I am in your house, I feel better already." Stuttering, she told him, "It is h—horrible what is going on in the c—chateau. They k—killed the poor footmen, cut off their h—heads."

"You poor child," Yves said in a soothing tone, rubbing her shoulder and back with one hand. "Go upstairs and crawl in bed with the girls. If anyone comes looking for you, I'll just tell them you are my daughter."

"*Merci,* Yves, *bonne nuit*"

Annise took the candle from Yves and made her way up the steps, that were little better than a ladder, into the loft under the thatched roof where her friend Eva and her little sister shared a bed. She removed her cape and sturdy leather shoes, blew out the candle and crawled into the bed. The girls gave a small moan as they were pushed together.

Annise lay in the dark, every muscle tense. *Pray, I must pray. Heavenly father, help me in this time of peril. Help Mama and Papa and keep them safe. Let the mob be gone and I return to the chateau in the morning and my parents will greet me and we eat breakfast together. Bless dear Yves and his family, whom I love. And the king and queen and dauphin and princess who are in a cold prison. I pray for them, let them be released soon. Thy will be done, but most of all give me courage to accept the hand fate deals me.*

In conclusion she recited the Lord's Prayer in a whisper, and sleep overcame her.

ᗫᗣᗧ

Count Peter de Brisson sat in his three-wheeled chair in silence. Azelma was able to set a side chair next to him, and she too was silent, holding his hands while they were surrounded by shouts and laughter and the clatter of fine china being broken. Outside the front door stood a tumbrel to which the count's favorite riding horse had been hitched. The wagon was loaded up with wine, food, and silverware, along with anything else someone fancied to take away. It was close to dawn when the old woman who had proclaimed herself queen put her face close to Azelma, gave a hiccup, and, with a big smile showing her rotten teeth, asked, "Where is the girl?"

"She is outside relieving herself. She will return soon."

"Good, because we are all going to Paris. My carriage is waiting."

"Yes, we will let you ride in the carriage with us."

"I and my friends ride the carriage. You walk."

"But my husband has a broken leg. He cannot walk."

"He has a nice chair with three wheels and you to push him."

Countess Azelma gave the woman a blank look then forced a smile. "You are right, the walk will be good."

A gray dawn appeared from the eastern sky as quite a parade made their way to Paris. At the head of the procession was the open carriage with the old lady called the queen. She was surrounded by young and old women attired in Azelma's fancy dresses. They had found her rouges and applied them to excess, giving their faces a nightmarish appearance. Following the carriage was the count in the wheelchair pushed by his wife.

Peter worried. *What will become of the horses they so roughly hitched to the carriage? My dear Azelma, I wish she would have escaped with Annise. That poor child needs the protection of her mother. Azelma just is too loyal of a wife. If it wasn't for this cursed leg, things might be different.*

Azelma struggled with the wheeled chair, especially where some snow lay. The snow clung to the wheels and jammed up. Peter would rise, hop on one leg and help her clean the wheels. Once they were clean again, he wrapped the wool cloak tightly around himself and sat down again.

One young man saw her struggle and helped Azelma clean the wheels. When they reached a small hill, he even helped her to push the count.

"*Merci,*" Azelma said. *Am I doing the right thing?* she wondered. *Maybe I should have fled while I had the chance. Poor Annise, all alone in the world. But abandoning Peter, I just cannot bear that thought. I could not live without him. He is my man, my reason for living, my love. I might die with him, but I don't want to live without him. Do I love him more than my daughter? I believe I do. She is strong. She was promised in marriage at eighteen, that means she would leave us anyway. She will become a wife and live far away.*

"How are you doing, Azelma, my love?"

"All is well with me. This nice young man here is helping me push the chair with wheels. Besides that, this exercise is good for the waistline."

"That's my girl," said Peter with a chuckle. "Looking at the bright side of the situation."

Chapter 2

January 21, 1793, Paris, France:

The man, in his early fifties, wrapped the green wool cloak tightly around himself to ward off the cold January air. More people than usual were in the streets that night. He observed large numbers in the Tuileries Gardens, sharing wine in an obvious mood of celebration. The call of *Vive la Republique* was heard over the singing of the *Marseillaise.*

How I hate that song. A vulgar song for vulgar people.

"*Allo,* Henri! Wait, Henri, wait for me!"

He turned around and saw his young friend Eduard Saulnier running after him.

"Eduard, what are you doing here?"

"I have come looking for a drinking companion. It seems all of Paris is out drinking tonight. Two-thirds are celebrating, and one-third are drowning their sorrows."

"Come with me. I will buy a bottle of wine, and we shall share it."

The two well-built men proceeded to the nearest tavern. The young bar-wench brought the wine and gave young Eduard a flirtatious look before she left with the sizable tip Henri squeezed into her hand.

"To your health," Eduard said.

Both men emptied their glasses quickly and poured more.

"To the end of an era," Henri said as a salute for the second glass. "May God protect us and France."

The tavern had been crowded when the two men entered. Now the table next to them was empty.

"Eduard, my young friend, you are in bad company. See, the table next to us is bare, and the people at the other two tables are leaving too. Here comes the landlord, and he will ask me to leave."

"Monsieur Sanson," said the portly tavern keeper with a sheepish look. "I hate to do this, but I need to make a living. As you can see, you are driving my patrons away. One would think, all these people would hail you as their hero, but you know how people are. Would you please take your wine and drink it somewhere else?"

"Don't feel bad, landlord, my friend and I were just

leaving." Giving Eduard a pleading look, Henri said, "I hope you do not mind coming home with me, I need someone to talk with. My poor wife has heard me lament so many times I know exactly what she will say."

"I am honored to go with you. Lead on, my friend."

The two men walked in silence to the Allee du Bourreau and stopped at the lone stone house.

Henri unlocked the leather covered oak door decorated with iron studs. "Come in, my friend. But before we go upstairs, let me show you the latest addition to my collection. Henri locked the front door and lit a whale oil lantern illuminating a large room with a high ceiling.

The first thing Eduard noticed was some five-foot-long wicker baskets stacked in a corner. "Once these crates are gone, the victims will not even have the dignity of a coffin," Henri said with a quivering chin.

They walked along the wall displaying a collection of swords, axes, a section of an ancient pillory, and an assortment of lengths of ropes. Many were stained, and all had tags with names and dates.

Henry reached for a burlap bag and untied it. "Here is the latest and most precious addition to the museum of my family's legacy."

Very carefully he pulled out the heavy metal object.

Eduard whistled. "So this is it. The blade that brought a thousand year dynasty to an end."

"I will never use this blade again. No one deserves to

be decapitated with the blade that finished *Him*."
Solemnly, Henri Sanson put the large blade back into the
bag. "I met him twice. Both times we talked like you and
I are now doing."

"Go on, Henri, tell me about him."

"The first time I saw Louis the Sixteenth was when I
petitioned him to change the title of my profession. He
gave me permission to no longer call myself the
Bourreau de Paris but the *Executeur des Judgements
Criminels*. We talked, and I told him that my family had
been executioners since the sixteenth century. All other
professions were closed to me. My uncle tried becoming
a locksmith, but he failed. No one would patronize the
business of a former *bourreau*. Do you know what the
word *bourreau* is defined as?"

Before Eduard could answer in the affirmative, Henri
continued, "Executioner or hangman, brute, inhuman
wretch, man without feelings. Me, without feelings? I,
who consider myself a refined and sensitive man. Am I
not a good husband and father? Am I not a good
neighbor, who helps the poor and sick? I know more
about herbs and body functions than any physician.
People call on me when they are sick and desperate. The
state calls upon me when they have wretches to dispose
of. But no one calls on me to help them celebrate
Christmas or share a glass of wine, save you, my friend.
No one lets me see their daughters get married or
celebrate a christening."

Henri pulled a napkin out of his pocket and dabbed his eyes. "I am well paid, but I'm a prisoner to my profession. Do you know what *he* told me? The king said that he is just as much a prisoner to his profession. He said that he would rather have been a clockmaker than king. Unfortunately, he had no choice about his job either. He was born to become king, just as I was born to become an executioner. He shook my hand. We two had much in common. The king made life and death judgments, and I carry out such decisions.

"Now, I feel like a murderer. I killed him. I robbed his family of a father and husband. The royalists are in mourning. He was a good king. I grant you, he was not a great king, but he was kind and good. Meeting him, I felt I had a friend."

Seeing tears in Henri's eyes, Eduard quickly asked, "When did you meet him for the second time?"

"Oh, that was only a few months ago. Dr. Guillotine consulted me about the design of an instrument for decapitation. I gave him practical advice, how a prisoner can best be laid. The doctor and I went to see the king. It was *he* who suggested the blade be angled like this," he said, drawing an angle with his hand and arm, "to ensure a quick, clean cut. Can you imagine, our king helping to design the instrument of his own end? Our king—now he is dead. I hope he did not suffer much. He was a good man. I liked him. I killed him."

Eduard saw tears roll down his friend's face. "Come,

I have gotten mighty thirsty. Where is that wine you promised me?"

"Forgive me, I am a terrible host. Come upstairs where it is warm. We shall drink the chill off our bones and soul."

The two men climbed the stone steps and entered a warm, comfortable apartment. In the parlor in front of a fireplace sat Henri's wife, Olive Sanson. She was knitting.

"Madame Sanson, we are fortunate to have a visitor tonight," said Henri, entering the room. "You remember Eduard? He went to school with our Gabriel."

"Of course, I remember him," Olive said. "He was our son's only classmate who dared come home with him. Good to see you again, Eduard."

Eduard gave the seated lady a hug and touched both her cheeks with his. "It is wonderful seeing you looking so well."

"*Merci.* What are you doing these days?"

"I finished the university and am now a land surveyor and map maker."

"That is a good profession," Henri said, while opening a bottle of wine. He took three glasses out of the ornately carved oak cupboard and started pouring. Handing glasses to Olive and Eduard, he raised his own in salute and said, "To France and to all of us. May God have mercy."

"Have you had any correspondence from Gabriel recently?"

"Yes," said Henri, cheering up. "Our son will be returning to Paris soon. He was working in Marseillaise, but with all the business here, I sent for him."

"There is just no need for my profession in Paris, or anywhere else I know of in France," Eduard said. "I make a little money drawing caricatures for the various newspapers in Paris. What I'm thinking of doing, is going to America."

"America?" said Olive, wide-eyed. "That is hardly a nation."

"At the moment, it is more of a nation than France," Eduard continued. "Only problem is, if I go, I want to be married. I hear there are many men for each woman there. I just don't know many young women, and the ones I do know, none please me enough to marry them."

"I don't know where you can find a suitable girl in these days," Olive said. "But they are about somewhere. I hope you meet one soon because I would love to go to a wedding. Promise to invite us." She took a sip of wine and with a faraway look continued. "You just must find the perfect woman. I pray you do."

"Thank you very much for your hospitality and prayers," Eduard said, setting his empty glass on the table. "I really have no right to marry, since my income is very small. I will go home and draw some more caricatures tonight, and tomorrow I start looking for a wife."

Eduard bid farewell to the Sansons by giving each a hug and cheek-to-cheek touch.

Henri accompanied his friend to the door and watched him head up the street. He looked up at the sky and stars. *Such a peaceful sky looking down at all the turmoil and evil below. Take care, my young friend. May you find your love and happiness. I wish the same for my dear Gabriel. May he too be able to escape this cursed profession. For me, it is too late. I will be an executioner until the day I die.*

Chapter 3

Annise woke as the first rays of dawn slowly illuminated the farmer's cottage. She heard Yves and his wife, Coulette, quietly moving about and dressing. Ives went outside. After a while, he returned and spoke softly to his wife. Annise crawled out of bed and to the edge of the loft floor so she could see the two people. She could not hear the whispers but could see Yves was shaken and Coulette silently crying.

Tears came to Annise's eyes, thinking of her dear, beautiful mother and tall, handsome father in who knows what condition in some filthy prison in Paris. *I shall never forget last night as long as I live. Those poor footmen, they were brothers and such gentle men. They would do anything for me. I remember the time my dog died, the one dog that was my own. I was only ten years old, and they played hide and seek with me. They played with me until the butler caught us. I had to plead with him and father not to dismiss them from our service. Poor Mere and Pere, where are they now? Please God, protect them. Mere told me to get myself to Aunt Melina, and she would protect me and give me shelter. I wish I would have appreciated my life in our chateau."*

Annise put on her shoes, reached for her cloak, and climbed down the steps into the main room of the cottage.

"*Bonjour* Mademoiselle Annise," Coulette said. "Were you able to get some sleep?"

"*Oui*, I slept a little. Have you been to the chateau yet, Yves?"

"*Oui*, mademoiselle. I urge you do not go there. Some Jacobian guards are stationed in front already. I need to get you out of here as quickly as possible. Where shall I take you?"

"I am to go to Madame Melina Dupin in Chateau de Partie. She is related to my mother."

"Yes, I know the way," Yves said. "I shall hitch my farm cart and put on some hay, in case you need a hiding place. But since you are dressed like a peasant, you look like one of us. Let me dirty the dress some for you."

Annise took a step back. "No, please don't. Suppose I just put a dirty apron on, would that not suffice?"

"I have an apron that needs to be washed," Coulette said.

She retrieved it from a corner and handed it to

Annise who put it on over her clean white apron and tied it at the waist.

"Now, do I look like I have been working?"

At that moment, Eva and her sister came down the steps, still wearing their nightgowns.

"Annise, what are you doing here so early?" Eva asked.

"I came last night and slept in bed with you."

"And I did not even know it. Is something wrong?"

"Yes, everything is wrong," Yves interjected. "Say *adieu* to your friend. She has to get away."

"Why, Papa?" Eva started crying, seeing the alarm on her father's face.

Yves quickly stepped outside and hitched up the two-wheeled cart. Meanwhile, Coulette sliced some bread and cheese for the travelers to take. Annise and Eva hugged each other, both crying. Eva's ten-year-old sister just watched with a questioning look.

"Adieu, my friend, and *adieu, Soeur."* Annise always referred to the little girl as Sister.

Annise wrapped the cloak around herself, took the food from Coulette, gave her a cheek-to-cheek hug, and stepped outside, where Yves was concluding the hitching of his horse to the cart.

A short way from the house was forest, and soon the cart was out of sight from not only the farmhouse, but also the Chateau de Brisson.

The young horse galloped for a long time at a brisk pace before it started walking.

Yves and Annise did little talking for several hours as they headed toward her new home.

They drove along a row of high hedges ending in an imposing gate of stone columns with a wrought iron arch containing the words *Chateau de Partie.* Yves reined the horse through the gate onto a long tree-lined road. When they finally saw the palace ahead, both of their jaws dropped, and their mouths stood open.

"*Mon Dieu*," is all Annise could utter. "I had no idea I would be living here. This place is immense."

"You have never been here?"

"A long time ago, when I was still small, we came to visit. I just don't remember it being that big. I hope my aunt is still alive and living here."

"We shall soon find out."

Annise removed the dirty apron while Yves pulled the cart in front of the palace. A guard in a maroon and gold uniform asked what their business might be.

"This young lady here is related to Madame Dupin, and she is asking for shelter."

"Can she not talk?"

"Yes, I can talk, I was just speechless. Is my Aunt Melina well and still living here?"

"Yes, she is here. Whom shall I say wants to see her?"

"I am Countess Annise de Brisson," Annise said

quickly. "The revolutionaries have raided our chateau, and my dear parents have been taken away."

"That is more information than I need," said the guard. Turning to a younger guard, he commanded, "Tell Madame Dupin another waif is seeking shelter. Her name is Annise de Brisson, Countess de Brisson."

"Oui, monsieur," said the guard with a salute before he went into the palace. Soon he returned and beckoned for Annise and Yves to enter.

They stepped into a large magnificent foyer, beyond anything Annise and Yves had ever imagined. The white marble floor had veins of shiny brass making intricate patterns. The walls that were not covered by mirrors with brass sconces were covered by Belgian tapestry depicting the pleasures of court life. Overhead was a gigantic chandelier containing hundreds of unlit candles. A wide and gracious marble staircase led to upper floors. A bright red carpet covered the steps.

Dozens of well-dressed young women stood either on the floor of the foyer or were looking over the railings from the second floor.

A tall lady in her upper eighties came out of a double door at the side of the reception hall, her white hair piled high on her head in a style rapidly going out of fashion, with long white corkscrew curls spilling onto the forest green silk dress.

With a straight back and head held high, she walked toward the newcomers and looked at them as if they were an undesired insect she was ready to squash.

Please, God, help me. Let her like me and take me in. Holy Mary, Mother of God, watch over your humble child.

"Now refresh my memory," said the old lady, "Exactly how are we related?"

"My mother told me her grandmother, Countess Marie de Chavous, was your sister."

"Ah, yes, the snooty sister who looked down on me because I married a commoner. See where I live now," she said with a wave of the arm. "I understand Marie went to her reward a long time ago."

"Yes, Aunt Melina, I hope I may call you that. I never knew my mother's grandparents."

"What is it you seek, young lady?"

"The revolutionaries have raided our chateau and arrested my dear parents. Mama told me you would shelter me. I beg of you that she was correct."

Melina saw the fear and pleading in the girl's large blue eyes. Her critical gaze softened. "How old are you?"

"I am seventeen until this coming April."

"A wonderful age to be. Of course, I will give you shelter. Who is the man with you?"

"He is farmer Yves Laseur. He is the top man on our estate. He is wonderful with the crops."

"Where do you live, farmer?"

"I have a house on Count de Brisson's estate, where I live with my family."

"If the Jacobians evict you, come here, I can always use a good farmer."

"Thank you, madame," Yves said with a bow of the head.

"Before you leave, go downstairs into the kitchen, and tell the cook to give you something to eat."

"Merci encore, madame, you are more than kind." Yves turned to Annise, "Take good care of yourself, mademoiselle. I am sure your parents will be released soon. *Au revoir."*

Annise felt like giving the man she had known all her life a hug but did not want to break protocol in front of her aunt and everyone watching. She just said, *"Au revoir,* Yves," and watched him follow a boy down the steps to the kitchen.

Madame Dupin gave the girl standing before her a close inspection. *Pretty thing, I must admit, but now that she is here, she needs to blend into her surroundings. That short peasant skirt will not do. The cape looks heavy the way it hangs from the shoulder. If her parents had the least foresight, I wager it contains wealth.*

"I imagine you rushed away without bringing anything else to wear with you."

"Oui, madame, just the clothes I am wearing."

"I will need you ladies," Madame Dupin called in a raised voice, "to find something in your trunks that will fit our new guest, Annise. Welcome to Chateau de Partie, young lady. My other guests will make you feel welcome."

Annise felt as if a boulder had suddenly fallen off her heart. She felt tears well behind her eyelids and wanted to give the old lady a hug. All she could do was stammer, *"M—Merci, merci b—beaucoup."*

"Celeste, why don't you take Annise upstairs and give her the room next to yours. See to her comfort and tell her my house rules."

"Oui, madame," said the pretty dark-haired Celeste, making a small curtsy. She took Annise's hand and led her up the stairs to a long red-carpeted hall with rooms on both sides. She opened a door and escorted Annise into the room. "I hope you will be comfortable here."

"Merci, Celeste, this is beautiful," Annise said, looking at the large bed with only four tall posts and no canopy. The walls were covered with flocked light green wallpaper and, in the marble fireplace, wood was piled neatly over some wrinkled up newspaper.

"It is cold in here," said Celeste. "I will light the fire." She picked up the silver striker laying on the mantle and after several strikes produced the spark that ignited the newspaper. "After this, the servants will tend to the fire."

"I know servants stay out of sight, but where do they enter the room?"

Celeste went to an armoire against the window wall, opened the double door, and showed Annise the stairs leading down. "These go to a tunnel through which the servants travel."

"My aunt spoke of house rules. What are they?"

"Breakfast you can either order for your room or go to the dining room where it is on the buffet. Lunch also is served buffet style in the dining room between noon and one. For dinner at seven, we all sit at the dining room table, and we dress. And I mean, we dress. You look like my clothes will fit you. I will lend you a dress. Otherwise you will starve. Also, Madame Dupin is a famous hostess. We have many gala evenings here and entertain the important people of France. We ladies are all to treat our guests with special admirations."

Annise wondered what exactly special admirations meant, but was afraid to ask. She feared the answer.

"Are you hungry? If you are, I can send for something."

"No, but I feel very fatigued. That bed looks very inviting."

"Then take a rest while I find something for you to wear. I shall bring it to your room."

"*Merci beaucoup*," Annise said, trying hard to keep a smile on her face.

Celeste, who was only two years older, seemed to understand the girl's situation and gave her something she desperately needed—a long hug—while stroking her hair.

Feeling the love and warmth from her new friend

released the dammed water, and tears flowed freely down her cheeks.

"It will all be well, my dear. We have the bad times to make us appreciate the good ones. Now lay down and get some sleep. The world looks brighter after you rest."

"What brings you here?"

"That is a long story we can talk about another time," said Celeste, suddenly turning away. "Now rest while I gather some dresses." She quickly left the room.

I better be careful what questions I ask around here. Annise took off her shoes, followed by her white apron and full red wool skirt. Next, she unlaced the black vest and laid it on a chair on top of the other garments and crawled into bed.

"Ah what luxury. Only one night sleeping on Yves's bed makes me appreciate good bedding. Poor Mama and Papa, where are they resting their weary bodies? Oh, Lord, help them."

Chapter 4

Eduard was awakened by the sun shining in the one small dormer window of his room on the fourth floor. He rose, relieved himself into the enameled chamber pot, and quickly dressed. He took the caricatures he had drawn the day before and gave them a close inspection. By the light of the sun, he filled in minor details that could not be seen by candlelight. Next, he took his chamber pot and carefully made his way down the staircase of the apartment house. Holding his breath, he emptied the pot onto the soil in the small yard in the back.

"There, that should help the bushes to grow," he said to himself and hurried back upstairs.

He checked in his cupboard and found a hard roll

and some cheese. Consuming that satisfied his hunger. He took the drawings, put them into a flat canvas bag, and left the house. He walked through the narrow streets to a wide boulevard and entered a building that contained several businesses, among them the revolutionaries newspaper called *Le Pere Duchesne.* He located the editor and showed him his artwork.

"*Bon, tres bon,* we can use them all. You are my best artist. I have a special assignment for you."

The editor, a gray-haired man with a neat mustache and goatee, looked at Eduard critically. "Do you have better clothes to wear?"

"At the moment, this is my best. I am saving my money to get a suit made. Why?"

"Robespierre has asked me to send an artist, along with himself and Louis de Saint-Just, to a soirée at the Chateau de Partie late next week. I will send you, provided you have the proper attire."

"If you pay me today, I can go to the tailor and remedy the problem."

"Come into my back room, and I will pay you."

Eduard followed him to a cubicle in the corner. The editor took a ledger and added up what he owed. He stooped down, unlocked a strong box, and took out some coins. "Here are eight *reales*," he said, handing the young man royal silver coins. "Please sign the ledger that you received the money."

"Gladly," Eduard said, taking the feather and dipping

it into the ink. "That should get me some fine clothes. Anything in particular you want me to concentrate on at the Chateau de Partie?"

"In general, the notables there, and of course, the famous hostess, Madame Dupin."

"I shall arrange for you to ride out there with Robespierre and Saint-Just. I will give you the details when I see you next week. Meanwhile, get more Paris street scenes, you know what I mean."

Yes, Eduard did know what he meant. His sentiments leaned toward the royalists, but money was money, and he was willing to work for any side that paid him. He tipped his tri-cornered hat containing a red, white, and blue rosette, and took his leave. When he approached the doorway to the street, the opening was darkened by a tall man. The man spoke in a friendly voice.

"Eduard, my friend, how wonderful to run into you."

"Gabriel," Eduard said while giving the man a hug. "I did not know you are in Paris."

"Only arrived yesterday, and today my father has me helping him doing his job."

"I thought you were trying to get out of the family business."

"I managed to work at the docks in Marseillaise hauling cargo," Gabriel said with a sigh, "but that was not far enough away. Before long, someone recognized me and spread the word. Soon I was dismissed from that job.

The only alternative I had was to return to Paris and help my father. He hates his job and I too, am doomed to it."

"What brings you to the newspaper?"

"I have a list of names of the people we beheaded this morning. I bring it to be published in tomorrow's paper. What brings you here?"

"I work for this paper drawing caricatures," Eduard said with a frown, biting his lower lip. "Could you let me see the list?"

Gabriel handed him the paper and watched his friend read the names. When Eduard looked up with relief, he just commented, "No one you know, I suppose."

"No, thank the Lord. I hope we can meet soon and catch up on events. Now I have to go to a tailor and get measured for a new suit."

"By the tone of your voice, I hear you have an important event coming up. Is there a wedding in your near future?"

"No, unfortunately not. But I am to go to a soirée with Robespierre and Saint-Just to Chateau de Partie next week. At the moment, I am dressed in my finest," he said, pointing with his thumbs to his worn red jacket.

"Oh, how I envy you, my friend. To go to an event in a palace. All such pleasures are closed to me, because of who I am."

"I see you as a kind, intelligent young man, who has an unfortunate job, through no fault of his own," Eduard said, placing a hand on his friend's shoulder. "Maybe you could wear a disguise and go with me."

"Why? Is it a costume party?"

"Unfortunately, it is not." Eduard took a long breath. "I really enjoyed seeing you, my friend. We have to meet again soon."

"Yes, you just have to come to my father's house after your event at the chateau, and tell us all about it. You know how lonely it gets. You are almost the only visitor."

"Give my greetings to your father and mother, and I promise to visit soon. *Adieu,* Gabriel.

"Adieu, Edward. Good luck at the tailors."

A short way from the newspaper was a tailor shop the editor had recommended. Eduard walked in and was greeted by a short, stooped-over man with a tape measure draped over his neck.

"Can you make a suit for me in five days?" Was the first question, after greetings had been exchanged.

"What fabric do you want the suit made out of?" asked the tailor with a smile.

"Wool mixed with silk, if you have it."

"I only have wool in dark colors. That is the latest style."

"You mean the old red coat I came in with is no longer the fashion?"

"No, monsieur, the darker more somber colors are in style."

"I suppose it goes with the times, dark and somber

times. Make my suit as fast as you can. I have a big event to go to in one week."

"I shall get it done. I have several girls sewing the seams." He pulled the curtain aside, and Eduard glanced into the back room where several ten to fourteen-year-old girls sat stitching the long seams. They looked up at Eduard and smiled, then lowered their heads and continued sewing.

While the tailor was measuring, Eduard took a critical look at himself in the long mirror. He was of medium height, but compared to the tailor he looked really tall. His head boasted a good crop of light brown wavy hair cut in the latest short style and without powder. His fawn brown eyes highlighted his handsome face.

He could not get his friend Gabriel out of his mind. *Poor man, he is such a good person, and fate has dealt him such a bad blow. We met in first grade when we were both six. For some reason, the other children immediately knew what job his father had, and they harassed him constantly. Hit him for no reason at all.*

I could not stand by and watch, so I came to his defense. I thank some of my uncles for teaching me how to fight. After I beat off some of the harassers, the others backed away. Gabriel and I became the best of companions.

I was honored to be invited to his house after school and do homework. It was there, I learned what a father is. Gabriel's parents are such wonderful people, and they treated me like another son. Too bad their other two children did not survive the first year. I will have to visit the Sansons soon, but first, I need to visit a lady.

"That is all I need for today," said the tailor. "Come back day after tomorrow for a fitting."

"Merci, et au revoir," Eduard said, heading into the street.

He bought a bouquet of flowers from a vendor and proceeded to a familiar house. He climbed one flight of stairs and knocked on an oak door with a discreet small sign *Rosalie Saulnier.*

"Who is it?" a voice asked.

"It's Eduard."

Soon the door opened, and an attractive middle-aged lady wearing a dressing gown stood there with a big smile and outstretched arms.

"Come in, my love, come in."

While they were embracing, a man stepped out of the back room. He put some coins on the table and bid adieu.

"Thank you," she said. "Have you met my son?"

"Oui, comment allez-vous?"

"Very well, thank you," said Edward. "And yourself?"

"Bien, merci." Looking at the lady, the man asked, "Next week at the same time?"

"Yes, I shall see you then," she said, escorting him out of the door. She turned to her son, "Eduard, how wonderful you visit. I was not expecting you so early.

Now, let me wish you all good things for your birthday."

"*Merci, Mere,*" he said, handing her the flowers. "A bouquet for the lady to whom I owe my life."

"Red roses in February, they must have cost you dearly. I think you are the only person who honors the mother on their birthday. Thank you so much." She went to the cupboard and took out a vase. At the kitchen sink, she pumped some water into it and set it on the table. "I made some cake yesterday. Would you like some now?"

"Provided you will eat with me," he said, looking at the woman in front of him.

She still looks good for her age. Forty, I believe. Her blonde hair hardly has any gray, and her figure is still voluptuous, not that bony, skinny look of many older women.

"*Mere,* today I am twenty-two. You promised that then, you would tell me the truth about my birth. I am here now, to listen to the story."

Rosalie set two plates with cake on the table, poured two glasses of white wine, and motioned for Eduard to be seated. She stared at the cake in front of her and took a deep breath. "Yes, today on the twenty-second of February 1793, when you turn twenty-two, is the right time for you to learn the circumstances of your birth. Enjoy the sweetness of the cake, while I tell you the story."

Eduard sliced off a piece with the fork and put it into his mouth. "Good, *Mere.*"

"As you know, I was the oldest of five children. My father was a shoemaker, barely earning enough to support the family. One of his customers was a marquis. There were times I accompanied my father to the marquis's palace, both for measuring the family's feet and to deliver the finished product."

"You helped your father in his business," Eduard said proudly.

"Oh yes, I did. My writing skills are limited, but I was good at shoe and foot drawings and filling in the measurements. I felt so important and educated when I had paper before me and a quill in my hands. That's how I was noticed by the Marques, Lady Noelle de Castellane.

"She took a liking to me and offered me a job as her lady's maid. Now mind you, a lady's maid is high on the scale of servants. I was sixteen and saw it the greatest opportunity of my life. The job meant I lived at the palace. I had my own room on the third floor, with my own bed. No sharing it with two sisters. It was utter luxury."

"I can imagine. How many children slept in one bed at home?"

"All three girls in one bed, the two boys in another. Lady Noelle was nice to work for. It was not long before their oldest son noticed me."

"Oh, oh, I can see where that is going."

"He was a handsome young man and charming as can be. Any girl would fall in love with him. He had the most wonderful brunet wavy hair and such sincere-looking brown eyes. On occasions, he would pass me a flower and a special treat to eat. We servants ate well, but simple food. The cooks would not let us have the fancy hors-d-ores they prepared for parties."

"Love goes through the stomach for a woman too then."

"Yes, my son." She chuckled. "Kisses soon followed. Not only that, but he hinted that I would make him a good wife."

"How old was he?"

"Seventeen. One evening he caught me on the back staircase as I was going to my room. He promised me a feast of sweetbreads in his room. At first, I refused, but he assured me no one would see me go there."

"And you went. I would too, in the same position."

"I was so overwhelmed by the opulence of his room, the canopy bed, the feast of expensive food washed down by champagne. He expressed his love for me and promised me as soon as he turned eighteen he wanted to get married. I need not go into any details, it was the first time of many. Of course, in public he never looked at me."

"I can understand that. Children are brought up with fairy tales of the handsome prince marrying the pretty commoner and living happily ever after," said Eduard with an understanding nod.

"Yes, it was a time of hopes and dreams. I believed

his promises and expressions of love. It took several months, and I became pregnant."

"Did you tell him, and how did he react?"

"I told him, and he expressed concern. Concern what his parents would say. He also said he was concerned about my health and believed we should no longer be intimate. After that, I hardly caught a glimpse of him."

"Did you tell anyone else?"

"Not at first. I kept you a secret until one day my lady noticed I was getting larger. I told her I was just eating too good. That worked for a while until one day she put both of her hands on my stomach and said, 'Just as I suspected. You are pregnant.' Then she wanted to know by whom. 'It's your son,' I said. 'Which one?' she asked."

"Yes, Mother, what is his name?"

"Marquis Hebert de Castellane."

"De Castellane? I'm a son of a marquis?"

"Yes, you are. How does that make you feel?"

"Should I feel any different? Yes, it is good to know who my father is, but tell me, what happened next?"

Rosalie was silent for a few minutes. Eduard could see her repress tears. He rose, put his arms around her shoulders, and kissed her on the head.

Finally, she continued, with a choking voice. "Lady Noelle dismissed me right away. I was too ashamed to go back home, as a fallen woman. I went to a convent and asked for asylum. The mother superior was very sympathetic and fought for me. To my surprise, she went with me to the palace and convinced the marquis, your grandfather, to do the right thing and give me a pension. It gave me enough money to live on and be able to send you to school. Every month the money came until you were twenty-one."

"But you had a business on the side," Edward said, sitting back down and taking a bite of cake.

"Yes, I really wanted to do better than just scrape by. Getting married was now out of the picture. No man wants a woman with a child unless she has money or property. When you were born, I fell in love with you the first second I saw you. You were now the reason for my living."

"Was I born in the convent?"

"Yes, you were. The mother superior had also sent for my parents who accepted me in spite of my condition."

"Yes, I can faintly remember my grandparents. Too bad they succumbed to pneumonia so young."

"I was looking to earn a bit of money when you were little. I tried sewing, but my talent does not go in that direction. I tried hat making, but the hats I made, no one wanted to buy. I had a lover or two then. Before long, one lover offered to buy me food or clothing or a toy for you. I thought, 'Why not, let them?'"

"I remember some of the *uncles*. Some of them were quite fatherly toward me. I was quite old before I knew what was going on. Let me assure you, *Mere,* I always respected you."

"Thank you, that means a lot to me. Through the years, I was able to lay a little money aside to live on in my old age. But with this inflation nowadays, I'm not sure anymore."

"Mere, do not worry. When you need someone, I am here."

"I do appreciate your concern, but I am realistic. One day you will take a wife, and she might not find it in her heart to take care of a former lady of the night."

"The girl I'll marry will love and respect you too."

"I hope so, son, I really hope so. Any prospects?"

"No, *Mere,* no one yet. But I hope to find one soon. Do you know any young ladies I should meet?"

"If I did, you would have met them already," Rosalie said with a far-off look.

Chapter 5

Annise was excited when she put on the new dress made especially for her. It was a light blue silk taffeta with a full skirt over a round hoop, the latest style. To achieve the desired cleavage, she balled up two handkerchiefs and pushed them under each breast. A maid styled her long blonde hair with back-combing to the desired height and added some blue silk flowers. Aquamarine earrings and a pendant were the only jewelry. Annise gave herself a final inspection in the full-length mirror and looked at her maid for approval.

"You look beautiful," said the girl, handing Annise a folding fan. "That color really emphasizes your eyes. No one at the ball will outshine you."

Annise left the bedroom and approached the top of

the wide staircase. She took her place in line with the other ladies, waiting for her name to be announced. As each lady's name was bellowed by the footman, she slowly descended the stairs and joined the gathering below. Finally, she heard, "Countess Annise de Brisson."

Slowly, she descended in the middle of the staircase. *Walk slowly and carefully, whatever you do, don't trip and fall. I would rather slide down the banister.* The thought of the picture that would make brought a big smile to her face.

Eduard had ridden with Maximilien Robespierre and Louis de Saint-Just in the carriage to the palace. The whole way, the two men discussed politics, hardly speaking to Eduard. They treated him as a hired hand, one not worthy of being gracious to. Once they had arrived, Eduard was busy making drawings on his pad of paper, while the two officials socialized with other guests. The party did not officially begin until all the ladies living in the palace had been announced and descended the grand staircase.

So many beautiful women in one place, thought Eduard, *that is almost beyond comprehension.*

He looked at his drawing pad and quickly sketched the staircase. When he looked up, he beheld the most exquisite creature he had ever seen. The vision in blue floated down the stairs and joined the sea of people. With his charcoal stick, Eduard drew quickly what he had just seen. Then he went searching for her among the crowd.

The musicians started playing dance music.

Annise found herself among people, many taller than herself. She noticed one tall young man with his back to her who looked familiar. She approached him from behind. "Marquis Lukas de Castellane?"

The man turned around and gave her a charming smile. "Sorry to disappoint you, mademoiselle, but I am Louis de Saint-Just, your humble servant."

"Not *the* de Saint-Just?" Annise said, wide-eyed.

"Yes, the one they call the Angel of Death. One and the same." Music was starting to play another song. "Would you do me the honor of dancing with me, Countess? It would give me great pleasure."

Annise looked at the tall and very handsome man before her. She had read about him in the newspaper and envisioned him to be ugly with horns on his head. She just stood there speechless while he took her hand and let her onto the dance floor where they joined another three couples, making a square. After a few notes of introduction, the dance music started, and the sets of four couples began a *contradans francaise*. At the conclusion of the dance, he bowed to her in appreciation, and she curtsied. Annise excused herself and quickly made her way through the ballroom to a glass double door out onto the patio, taking deep breaths of the cool, night air.

I can't believe I just danced with Saint-Just. Who would ever think he would be that handsome and charming?

"What are you doing out here, child?" It was her Aunt Melina. "Are you well, my dear?"

"Yes, Auntie, I am. Do you know I just met Louis de Saint-Just?"

"Yes, I saw you dance with him. Go seek him out, be nice to him, and you might be able to get your parents released. He and Robespierre are the best of friends, and those two, have the most influence in the Committee of Public Safety."

"Robespierre is here too? I have seen drawings of him, but I never noticed him here tonight."

"He is not very noticeable. He is slight of stature with a pale complexion and powders his brown hair. Come, I will introduce you to him."

The old lady took Annise by the hand and led her inside where the band was playing some background music. Melina headed straight to Saint-Just who stood next to Robespierre conversing with two other men. When the men saw their hostess, they ceased their conversation and greeted the women.

"Madame Dupin, you have outdone yourself tonight," said Robespierre. "What a wonderful party, and thank you for inviting us."

"It is my honor you came," she said. "I want you to meet my niece, Countess Annise de Brisson. Annise, this is our dear Maximilian Robespierre," she said, placing her hand on the thirty-five-year-old's arm. "And you already met his good friend, Louis de Saint-Just."

"*Enchante*," said Robespierre, taking her extended hand and kissing the air above it.

"The pleasure is mine," said Annise, touching the edge of the hand-held fan with her fingers.

"You may call me Maxi," Robespierre said, reading her hand signal. "Would you care to step out onto the patio? Do you want to join us, Louis?"

"Be happy to."

The two men took their leave from Madame Dupin and accompanied Annise outside. Saint-Just took his handkerchief, spread it on a concrete bench, and motioned for Annise to sit. Both men sat on either side of her.

"What is it, mademoiselle you want to discuss?" Robespierre asked.

"It concerns my parents. They were seized out of our chateau and forced to march away by the mob. My father had a broken leg and was in a chair with wheels at the time. That was early in January and, since then, I have not heard from them or been able to find out where they are." Tears came to her eyes. "Please, kind gentlemen, I am so worried about them. Could you possibly tell me where they are, and let them write to me? What would even be better, and I would do anything for it, would be if you can get them released." Big tears rolled down her cheeks, and she spoke with difficulty. "I am still seventeen and a virgin. But if I could please you, gentlemen, I would sacrifice my maidenhead to you for the life of my parents."

Robespierre looked at his young friend de Saint-Just, with a knowing smile. The two men reached for each other's hands behind her back and gave a simultaneous squeeze.

After a while, Robespierre put his hand on her shoulder and spoke in a soft voice and furrowed brows. "My dear Countess Annise, that is a generous offer you make, but I am not interested in taking your maidenhead. This I promise. I will see to your parents' comfort. That is all I can do. What do you say, Louis? Can we help this lovely young lady?"

"I will not interfere with the committee. Maybe we can just postpone their trial for a while."

"But, monsieurs, if what I read in the newspaper is true, you are the most influential members of that august body," Annise pleaded with more tears than ever running down her cheeks.

"I hate to see a lady cry," Robespierre said, giving her a clean handkerchief. "I promise to make your parents as comfortable as possible if you stop crying."

Annise wiped her eyes and looked at each man. "*Merci,* you both are so kind." She looked into Saint-Just's handsome face. *They call you the Angel of Death. Please, be a real angel and show mercy.*

The two men sat silently with Annise, while she composed herself. When the tears dried, and the pinkness had left her face, they escorted her back toward the ballroom.

A new dance was about to start. Robespierre smiled. "May I have this dance with you, Countess?"

"It would be my pleasure."

He extended his arm shoulder height and bent his elbow with the hand palm down. She gently placed her gloved hand on his, and they walked into the ballroom, followed by Saint-Just who asked a lady to dance with him.

The two couples joined another two pairs on the floor and completed another contra circle.

Eduard watched as Annise gracefully went through the steps of the dance, giving the other dancers charming smiles when they were paired. *There she is, the woman of my dreams. As soon as this dance is over, I will rush to her side and dance with her.*

When the dance was over, and the partners had bowed and curtsied to each other, Eduard rushed to her side and asked for the next dance.

"*Avec plaisir,*" she said with a bright smile.

"*Merci,* the pleasure is all mine, Countess."

"*Comment vous appelez-vous?*"

"My name is Eduard Saulnier, and I'm delighted to meet you."

A footman with a tray of champagne glasses walked by. Eduard took two and handed her one.

They looked at each other over the gold rim of the glasses. He studied her. *What a ravishing creature, with the most incredible blue eyes I have ever seen. Can a woman like that, even consider associating, with a poor man like me?*

She averted her gaze for a moment. *He is taller than I, but not so tall that I need to strain my neck to look into those wonderful fawn brown eyes. He looks at me as if I were the only woman in the room. What smooth even features, I'd love to run my fingers through his wavy hair. There is something about his presence that makes me feel safe. Can this be love?*

I'm in love with her, Edward decided. *I have heard the phrase 'love at first glance,' but now I know it is true. Lord, help me. Let her like me too.*

They clinked the glasses and drank, looking at each other. The music started playing. They set their glasses down and headed for the dance floor.

"You are a wonderful dancer," she told him when they again partnered in the figure of the dance.

"You, my lady, are grace and beauty yourself."

She blushed and lowered her eyes.

When the dance ended, he escorted her to a love seat. She moved her fan with her left hand.

"Are you telling me we are being watched?"

"Precisely. I am sure my aunt, the hostess, is wondering who you are and what brings you here. Would you like to meet her?"

"I would be honored."

They both rose and walked to the chair where her aunt was sitting, surrounded by royalists, Girondists, and Jacobians, including Robespierre.

"If only all of you could get along as well outside, like you do in my house," Melina said in a loud voice, "The world would be a better place."

"The king had to die so that the country can live," said Robespierre in a cold voice with his lids trembling over his green-gray eyes.

"Now, Maxi, enough political talk for tonight." Melina lowered her voice and said to him, "Do any of the ladies here please you? I'm sure they would be delighted to spend some time with you."

Robespierre gave a perfunctory look around the room and, returning his gaze to the old lady, graciously declined her generous offer.

"Aunt Melina," Annise said quickly when there was a pause in the conversation. "This young man would be honored to meet you."

"Madame, thank you for allowing me to be your guest. My name is Eduard Saulnier, and I work for *Le Pere Duchesne* and other newspapers. I do drawings for them."

"Wonderful, and welcome. When you do a drawing of me, please make sure I will look thirty—no, forty—years younger than I really am."

"Madame, whatever your age, you are still beautiful."

Melina held her fan to her lips. Eduard took her hand and kissed it.

"I see you are a gentleman since you know the language of the fan," Melina said with a big smile. "Is there something you would like to ask me?"

"Yes, do I have your permission to court your niece, Annise?"

"Can you come to coffee tomorrow afternoon for us to discuss it?"

"If you name the time, I will be there."

"Good, three in the afternoon then. Now you two young people go and dance and enjoy yourselves."

"Thank you, madame, *merci* Auntie," they said in unison and joined the people starting another *contredanse*.

Chapter 6

Eduard rented a horse and rode, often at a gallop, to the Chateau de Partie. When he entered the gate, he looked at his silver pocket watch and timed his speed to allow him to arrive at five minutes before three. The guard at the door of the palace whistled for a stable boy to take the horse to be watered and fed. Eduard brushed the dust off his new dark suit and entered the foyer. The magnificence of the building was even more impressive in daylight. He stood next to the footman and kept his eyes on the stairway, thinking of the beautiful sight he saw the evening before.

Melina Dupin descended the stairway. Again her hair was high on her head and decorated with egret feathers. Her dark blue dress dated from the time when there was peace in the land, and the king sat on the throne. With hoops on each hip, the bottom of the skirt was wider than many people were tall.

"You are punctual, young man, I like that. Did you have a pleasant ride out from Paris?"

"*Oui Madame*, I had a lively steed."

She gave him her hand, and he kissed the air above it. "Come into the library, we need to speak."

Two footmen opened the doors as they approached. The walls of the library were lined with shelves containing leather-bound books behind glass doors. In the middle of the room stood a round table, set with three cups and small plates. A plate in the middle of the table contained cake and petit fours.

"Come, take a seat. Annise will be with us in a little while."

When they were seated, a woman servant poured coffee. A wave of the old lady's hand made her hurry out of the room.

"Now, young man, I will come right to the point. What qualities do you have that give you the courage to ask to be able to court my niece, the Countess Annise de Brisson?"

"Madame, when I saw her for the first time descending the staircase, my heart stopped beating. When it started beating again, I knew Cupid had shot an arrow into it. It was an eternity later, before I had the opportunity to dance with her. Speaking with her, it was as if I had known her since birth. I am college educated and have the potential to earn a decent amount someday."

"I gather you are not nobility," Melina said picking up a piece of cake with a silver cake lifter and placing it on his plate. "Eat, and enjoy."

"*Merci, madame,* no, I come from a family of the middle class." *I hate to lie, but that is what I say when I meet someone new. Receiving good grades meant I received a scholarship to continue my studies in college. I finished my education just before the Revolution started when all the schools were unfunded. The poor young men nowadays have no college to go to. If they cannot afford to go abroad for schooling, they are out of luck.*

"Being of nobility is not of fashion in these times," she said, taking a small sip of hot coffee. "You might have noticed, I have no fancy title either, but you can see how I live. How do you support yourself?"

"I do caricatures and drawings for the newspaper and anyone else who needs them."

"Oh yes, I remember you telling me that last night. Is that enough to support a wife?"

"Barely, and certainly not a lady. I only laid eyes on Countess Annise last night and cannot get her out of my mind. I am absolutely smitten by that wonderful young woman. My biggest desire is to marry her and take her to America."

"America? A land that is hardly a nation."

"At the moment, they are more of a nation than

France. It is a land where everyone has opportunity to make something of himself."

"So we hear, far away. Truth at times gets lost in reality." Melina looked at him critically while chewing on a piece of cake. "Infatuation comes and goes quickly. It takes time for real love to grow. Tell me, what would you do to win her heart?"

"I know I would do anything for her, *anything*."

"I have guardianship of her at the present time, her mother is my grandniece. I have an assignment for you. If you are able to accomplish it successfully, then I will give you my blessings. I might even go one step further and say, that her parents will give their blessings also."

"Whatever the challenge, I will eagerly accept it," he said, leaning forward with his eyes aglow. "What is it you want me to do?"

Melina took another bite of her chocolate cake. With a nod of the head, she indicated for him to do the same. Eduard slowly ate some bites. Several minutes went by in silence. *I wonder what she wants me to do to test my sincerity? This is like a fairy tale where the prince had to pass several trials to get the princess. Lord, whatever she wants me to do, I know you will help me if she is the right woman to be my wife.*

The cake slice was half consumed when the old lady laid down her fork and gave Eduard an intense look. "How old are you?"

"I turned twenty-two just a few days ago on February twenty-second."

"Ah, to be that young again, and to know what I know now."

"Unfortunately, the two do not go together," he said with an admiring smile. "That is why it is a privilege to be in the company of someone wise like you, madame."

"You have a glib tongue, young man. Now my challenge for you to win dear Annise's favor is this…"

Eduard leaned forward with anticipation.

"Both of her parents, the Count and Countess de Brisson have been seized by the revolutionists and are in prison. We do not know where. Your assignment is to get them out of prison. Once they are safe, I will give you my blessings to marry the young lady."

Eduard leaned back, feeling the blood drain from his face. He could not speak. Finally, after a long minute, he stammered, "H—How do you expect me to do that?"

"That, young man, is totally up to your wiles. If I knew how it could be done, they would be free by now. I suppose you would like to visit with Annise now."

"*Oui*, madame."

She picked up a brass bell and rang it. The footman entered and bowed his head.

"Bring in Mademoiselle Annise and more hot coffee."

The footman bowed his head and left the room. Soon he returned with the coffee and Annise. Eduard rose quickly. Slowly Melina rose and approached the girl.

"My dear, come and have some coffee and talk with Eduard. I have some other business to attend to. It was a pleasure talking with you, Monsieur Saulnier. My hope is, we see each other again soon."

"The pleasure was all mine," he said as she left the room. He extended his hand to Annise. She reached for it with her palm down, indicating an expected hand kiss. He gently took her hand and kissed the air above it saying, "It is a pleasure to see you again."

Annise gave him a coy smile. "Thank you for coming. I see Aunt Melina is giving us her blessings."

"*Oui*, for that I am grateful to be able to see you today. She also gave me an assignment or challenge I need to overcome in order to keep courting and eventually marry you."

"Oh," she said with her eyes wide. "What might that be?"

"I am to get your parents out of prison any way I can."

Annise gasped. "If you could do that, I would be the best wife anyone could wish for." She reached for his hands, and tears came to her eyes. "Can you possibly do that? I hear, every day more people lose their heads, and I'm afraid my parents are next." She took both of his hands and knelt in front of him. "Oh, Eduard, if you could help them, you would have my undying love and admiration."

He raised his arms to help her to her feet. "My dear Annise, you do not need to kneel in front of me as if I was a god."

Once again standing, she hugged him. Her pink rosebud lips were close to his face. As if pushed by an unseen power, he put his lips on hers and kissed her. Only a small feathering kiss before he pulled his head back. She reached behind his neck with both hands, pulled his head close to hers, and opened her lips in anticipation. He kissed her again then gently pushed her away. He could feel desire stirring within him and knew this was not the time or place to answer that desire.

Both sat close to each other at the table and began sipping coffee. "I will do everything in my power to help your parents," he said. "I don't know yet how, but I will think about it, and I have a friend who might be able to help."

"Thank you so much for the hope you are giving me. I will dream of the time my parents are free again, and I will be your wife. I will go anywhere you want, and always be faithful and admire you."

"Would you be willing to go to America with me?"

"To America, to China, wherever my husband goes, I would happily follow."

A footman opened the double door from the foyer, and Aunt Melina entered. "Young man, if you wish to reach Paris before dark, you better leave now. Your horse is waiting."

"Oui, madame, and thank you for allowing me to visit."

"How do we best communicate with you?" Melina asked.

"Every day I go to the *Le Pere Duchesne* newspaper. I can get messages there."

"We will write to you there, when we need to reach you," said Melina, extending her hand, thumb up. He shook it and she left the room.

"I too thank you for the visit and wish you success in your quest," said Annise, extending her hand, palm down.

He held it gently and kissed it, touching the back of her hand. Unwilling to let go, he glanced around the room. The footman was tending to the fire in the marble fireplace. Quickly Eduard reached for her upper arms and kissed her on the lips. "I will do my utmost to get your parents out of prison," he whispered. "Even if it should cost my life."

Annise sucked in the air and held her breath, "Oh, Eduard, you are the most amazing man I ever met. God bless you and keep you safe. *Adieu* until we meet again. I hope it is soon."

"Each second away from you will be torture, but go I must, I now have a purpose. *Au revoir,* until we meet again." He turned around and quickly left the room.

Annise went to the window and watched him mount

the horse and ride off into the gray afternoon. *I don't know what it feels like to be in love, but I have this painful, happy feeling inside. Is that love? If he is sincere about working on my parent's release, he must really love me. My lips still tingle from the kiss. Now I understand Mama's feeling for Papa. I hope my love and eventual marriage will be as good as theirs has been all these years. Where are they now? Please, Lord God, let me get a letter from them. Let them be released. I know you are busy, but would you take just a little time and answer my prayers?*

Chapter 7

Countess Azelma heard her baby screaming. She ran to the nursery of the small palace and found baby Annise lying in her crib, with no one near her. There were no servants, no nanny, and no footman. *Where has everyone disappeared to?* She picked up the baby and held her in her arms. After a few whimpers, the baby was quiet and content. Suddenly, the countess sat on a cold floor cradling the baby in her arms and humming a tune.

A hacking cough suddenly woke Azelma. She realized she was not in the palace, but sitting on a cold stone and concrete floor with her back against the wall. In her arms, she was cradling her husband's head.

Count Peter de Brisson opened his gray eyes, looked

at his wife, and smiled. "Good morning, *cherri*, we have survived another night."

"I was dreaming I was home when Annise was a baby, and I held her in my arms. Had you not coughed, the dream might have lasted longer."

"My apology, *cherri*. I saw you were still sleeping, but the cough escaped me. Please, go back to sleep and pick up the dream where you left it, and include me too."

"I wish I could do more than dream of home," she said, putting on a bold face. "How are you feeling, my love?"

"The tightness in my chest is easing up." He looked around the cell they shared with five other men and women. The only light was a small barred window at eye level in the stone wall. The sanitary facility was a hole in one corner with an iron pipe, leading whatever was deposited to some unknown place. Once a day the bucket of water sitting next to it was emptied down the hole and refilled with fresh water by the jailer. A loud knock sounded on the heavy wooden door. The prisoners quickly roused themselves, grabbed their enameled mugs, and held them through a small hatch in the door.

"Breakfast is served," said Peter, looking at his watery soup.

"Thank you, Lord for our food," said the priest "*Bon appetit,* Brothers and Sisters in Christ."

After the morning meal, Count Peter looked out of the window and reported the weather to everyone in the cell. "The sky is fifty-percent blue and fifty-percent white and gray clouds. The easterly wind is crawling along at eight meters a minute. I predict, before the day is over, all of us will still be here, unless we have gone somewhere else."

"Let us hope, if we go somewhere else, it will be a better place," said the tall, gray-haired priest. "Anyone wishing to join me in prayer, please step into my corner."

The three men and three women clustered around the priest while he recited a long prayer. In conclusion, they sang some songs, while walking around in a circle. After an hour, everyone sat against the wall, except Peter who exercised his healing leg.

While he paced the floor, he told funny stories, either from his own experience or others he had heard. It made him feel good hearing his fellow prisoners laugh. Everyone suddenly roused, their bodies tense, when they heard the door being unlocked and the jailer step in.

"Citizens de Brisson, both of you, come with me."

"Where are we going?" Azelma asked, while getting to her feet.

"Come with me, and you will see," the jailer answered gruffly.

The count and countess wanted to give everyone a hug, but saw the impatience on the jailer's face and just gave everyone a wave with the hands while saying *au revoir.*

"*Au revoir*, God keep you until we meet again," said

the priest while the others nodded and waved. Peter and Azelma followed the jailer up the steps and out into a courtyard, where a rough horse-drawn wagon stood with a driver.

"Get in," ordered the jailer.

"It's too high for my wife to climb in," Peter protested.

The jailer grabbed Peter and forced him to his knees with his head close to the ground. Another jailer helped the countess step on her husband's back and climb in. After that, the count climbed in, followed by the jailer who tethered one wrist from each to the side of the cart. The driver shook the reins, and the two horses went out the gate onto the streets of Paris.

"Is this our end?" said a pale-faced countess, looking at her husband.

"I don't know," said Peter, reaching for his wife's hand, with his free one. "We are in God's hands."

"No, we are in the devil's hands," she said with furrowed brows and fear in her blue eyes.

"Courage, my dear. Do not give them the satisfaction of seeing us suffer. We will get through this dark tunnel and come out on the other side."

"Yea, though I walk through the valley of the shadow of death, I will fear no evil: for thou art with me, thy rod and staff comfort me," she whispered, and Peter finished reciting the psalm.

After about an hour, they saw the Temple Tower

ahead. The driver maneuvered the team into the secured yard next to the old castle. A young soldier approached them and said politely, "Welcome to your new home."

He placed a stool near the wagon and helped the couple get out. As they headed toward the imposing looking building, the wagon took off.

"We have a special room for you, Citizens," the soldier said as he let them up the spiral staircase with another soldier walking behind them. He opened a heavy wooden door and led them into a comparatively comfortable room. A wide bed stood against one wall along with a table and some chairs. A small window streamed in sunlight. In the next room was a primitive kitchen with a small wood stove and a water pump over a stone sink. A bucket and chamber pot was their comfort station.

"To whom do we owe the rise of accommodations?" Peter asked the young soldier.

"This was the room occupied by the king, but he does not need it anymore. The queen and two children are below here," he said, pointing at the wooden floor. "As you can see, there are pens and paper. You may write letters, and receive a visitor or two. You also can walk upstairs on the ramparts. Any other questions?"

"Yes," said Peter eagerly. "Do you have any idea why we were transferred? Not that I am complaining."

"It is my understanding that Robespierre himself saw to it."

"Robespierre, *the* Robespierre? I can hardly believe it," said Peter. "What do you say about that, Azelma?"

"I am without words," she said. "I wonder if Aunt Melanie might have been able to influence him. I have to write letters to both her and our dear Annise, and let them know where we are."

"I will be glad to mail letters for you," said the soldier. "I will leave you now." He left through the oak door but did not lock it.

"Just think, Peter, seven weeks ago, this would have been, to us, a very humble dwelling and now it seems luxurious."

"Yes, that shows you how spoiled we were. Now we will appreciate even the smallest blessings. I will write a letter to your aunt and thank her for taking good care of our daughter, while you compose a letter to Annise."

They sat at the small table, each with paper in front of them and dipping their quills into a glass jar of ink. Peter watched Azelma bite her lower lip in concentration as she was writing. When she looked up and saw him give her such a loving look, she looked at the bed. He followed her gaze.

"You want to?"

"Later," she said, "We have to take advantage of daylight and write the letters. After that, I need a good washing."

"I too need to wash first, but then—"

There was a knock on the door, and the same young

soldier brought in a tray with a pot of tea, some bread and cheese and a glass jar containing pickles.

"Something green to eat, how wonderful. I have been longing for anything that might be green," said Azelma, pushing the paper aside to make room for the tray.

"I will be coming in the morning with food. If your letters are finished, I can take them, but you will need to pay postage."

"Thank you, Citizen, we have a few coins," said Peter. "Do you have a name too?"

"Of course, I have a name." He chuckled. "It is Pierre, Citizen Pierre."

"And we are Citizens Brisson. We both wish you a peaceful night."

"*Bonne nuit,*" said Pierre and closed the door, locking it from the outside.

Peter and Azelma enjoyed every morsel as they ate by the fading light of day. They lit a candle and washed themselves with cold water, then went to bed and enjoyed each other's bodies, both crying out with pleasure.

The next morning, Pierre accompanied them down the spiral stairs into the garden enclosed by a high stone wall. Other prisoners were also outside. They noticed an old lady wearing a black dress with a girl in her early teens and an eight-year-old boy.

"Why would they have children in prison?" Azelma asked her husband.

"I think that is the queen and her children."

"No, that can't be," Azelma said, looking shocked. "The queen is only in her mid-thirties, that woman is at least fifty. Her hair is totally white, and that is not powder."

When they came face to face with each other, Peter wished the family *bonjour.*

"Yes," said the woman, "We must make the best of each day."

"Madame, let me introduce myself. I am Peter de Brisson, and this is my wife, Azelma."

"You are fortunate to have each other. You may call me Antoinette, and this is Charles and Theresa."

The girl curtsied, and the boy bowed his head, looking at Peter. "Would you play ball with me?"

"Don't be so forward," the queen reprimanded.

That is quite permissible," Peter said. "I shall be glad to play ball with you."

"Come, I have a ball hidden behind a bush." And the boy ran off, followed by Peter.

"That child really misses his father," the queen said with a sigh. "Would you like to join me on the bench over there? It is good to have someone to talk with."

"Of course, your highness, I'd be honored to."

"Just call me Antoinette. We are nothing more than prisoners."

"I understand we have the rooms occupied by your husband. Compared to the prison in Paris we were in, the Tower seems like a luxury."

"That must have been a really dismal place. I thought this place was bad. Of course, we came from Versailles to the Tuileries to here. Let's talk about happier times."

"Yes, I remember seeing you at masquerade balls in Paris a few times some years ago."

"Oh yes, we had fun then," said the queen with a far-off happy look.

When she smiled, her face dropped a good ten years. The princess quietly sat next to her mother and took her hand, as if to say, *all will be well again.*

The three ladies watched Peter and Louis Charles throw the ball to each other. At times the boy had to jump up to catch it. When he caught a high ball, Peter was generous with praises at how well the boy did. It made the child laugh.

"I am so happy to see my son laughing," said the queen. "I thank God for sending you to us. You are brightening our day."

"The last two months have taught us to really appreciate little things. Everyone should be more grateful."

"Outdoor time is over," called a grizzled-looking old guard. "Time to go back in."

The queen and princess rose with a resigned look and started toward the gray tower. "I hope to see you again, perhaps tomorrow."

"Let us hope so," said the countess.

The young prince ran to his mother. "We had fun, Mama. Can't I stay out longer?"

"We must do what the citizen tells us. Come, we'll play a board game inside."

He gave a small moan then brightened and gave Peter a wave. "We'll play again tomorrow, monsieur."

"I hope so, child, I really hope so."

Chapter 8

A few days later, Annise sat in a game room of the Chateau de Partie, playing cards with three other young ladies. Through the sheer curtains, she could see the mail courier approaching in his coach. When she saw him leave, she excused herself and headed for the console table in the foyer. Aunt Melina was already going through the mail. Annise stood quietly until she heard, "Here is a letter for you."

Her heart skipped a beat as she took the sealed envelope and looked at the name of the sender.

"It's from *Mere*," she called out, her face flushed with excitement.

"And a letter from your father is addressed to me." Melina continued sorting through the mail. "Another letter for you, *cherri*. Go and read them and share any news with me."

"Thank you, Aunt Melina," Annise said and hurried away.

"A lady does not run in the house," Melina called after her.

Without slowing the pace, Annise rushed into her room, threw herself across the bed, and opened the letter from her mother.

> *Paris, 6th of March, 1793*
>
> *Our Darling Daughter Annise,*
>
> *This is the first opportunity I have to write to you. I hope you are well, my cherri. Our condition has greatly improved yesterday. Up to then, we were in a small prison cell with ten other people to begin with. Five were taken away—to where, we do not know. When we left, five people remained behind. We now are at the Temple Tower, occupying two rooms once occupied by the king. We learned he was executed. A young soldier who is one of our jailers said the queen and two children live right below us. There might come a time we will be able to see them when we have the freedom to go outside.*
>
> *Your father made a good recovery with his broken leg and has not lost his sense of humor. Even in the dismal jail cell, he was able to bring*

laughter to all within earshot. We do not know why providence smiled upon us, by giving us better accommodations, but neither do we understand why we are in prison, to begin with. All we know is, France is coming apart at the seams, and someone needs to carry the blame for all the famine.

Politics has never been my favorite subject, and I will get to other matters. We will be able to have visitors. If you could possibly come, with a chaperone, of course, would you please bring us some clothes. We are still wearing the same clothes we left the chateau in. Even a cast off by a maid would be appreciated. We can also receive mail here, and any correspondence would be so treasured.

I will close now and give this letter to a soldier. Your father and I love you with all our hearts. Give my greetings to Aunt Melina and anyone else who knows us.

Love and Kisses, Your mere et pere.

Annise laid the letter on the table with a deep sigh. She opened the letter from Eduard.

Paris, the 8th of March, 1793
Dearest Highly Honored Countess Annise,
I hope this letter finds you in good spirits. This morning I learned your parents are now in the

Temple Tower. I understand their circumstances have greatly improved, but they are not out of danger. The fact is, they now have the attention of men high in the regime, which might even be to their detriment. I don't wish to frighten you, but those are the facts.

My mind is constantly thinking about them, and how I might be able to help. If you should come to Paris to visit them, please notify me. I would like to go with you and see what the tower looks like. No one I know has ever the seen the inside.

Most days I am at Le Pere Duchesne *newspaper on the Rue de la Glaciere from morning until late afternoon. To see you soon would mean I could breathe again. You cannot imagine how much being in your presence would mean to me.*

Your friend, Eduard

Annise took the letter from her mother and found her aunt in the game room, playing cards.

"Good news, my parents are no longer in a dismal little prison cell but in a room in the Temple Tower. *Mere* writes they will be allowed to receive company."

"Do you wish to share the letter with me and the ladies in the room here?"

"Yes, I do," Annise said, and she read the letter aloud to an eager audience of nearly a dozen women.

When she finished, Melina said, "You can take a

coach tomorrow morning and visit them. Ladies, why don't all of you gather some things to send along, to see to their comfort."

"What can we send?" asked a pretty red-haired distant cousin.

"Soap and perfume and any little things you would like to have, if you had nothing. I have some plain clothes I can send. Even some good things to eat would be appreciated. I shall have the cook prepare some delicacies for them. You can go with a woman servant besides the driver."

"Oh, Aunt Melina, you are so kind, *merci, merci.*" Annise dropped to her knees in front of the seated lady. "My parents will be so grateful. I love you, Auntie." She put her head on the old lady's lap.

Melina gave her hair a few strokes. "Come, ladies, let us find some things for the poor prisoners."

A short time later, Annise had a big bundle to take to her parents.

ⲟⳍⲟⳍ

Early next morning, Annise—with a middle-aged driver named Thibaut and his wife Sana—got into a coach for four with a roof and took off as soon as a gray dawn was breaking. As they traveled on the road along the Seine, Annise would have enjoyed the ride if the weather would not have looked so frightening. Big gray clouds threatened to release a downpour any second. When they reached the outskirts of the city, Annise shouted to Thibaut, "Please take me to *Le Pere Duchesne* newspaper on the *Rue de la Glaciere.*"

"*Oui, mademoiselle*, I know where that is."

Moments before they arrived at the building housing the newspaper and other establishments, the sky opened, and rain fell in large drops. Annise jumped out of the carriage and ran into the building. Thibaut took an oilcloth, threw it over himself, and talked to the horses in a calm voice. His wife remained dry in the carriage.

Annise found the newspaper, following a sign. She entered the office, and a young man inquired if he could assist her.

"I am looking for Eduard Saulnier."

"You are in luck, he was ready to step out, but stayed because of the rain." In a loud voice, he called, "Eduard, someone is here to see you!"

When Eduard saw her, his face brightened like sunshine on a snowy morning. "Annise, my dear, how wonderful to see you." He reached for her extended hand and kissed it. "What brings about this unexpected visit? Did you receive my letter?"

In almost a whisper she said, "Can you get away for a while? I am going to the Temple, and I hope you can come with me."

"I can do that, *cherri*, just as soon as the rain lets up," he held both of her hands. "Your hands are cold.

Come, wrap them around a cup of hot coffee."

"Thank you, I would like that." She went with him around the printing press to a stove with a pot of hot coffee. "I never knew coffee could taste this good," she said, looking over the rim of a ceramic mug. "I am so glad you will come with me to the Tower. I have quite a bundle of things to take to my parents."

"This rain should stop soon," Eduard said, looking out of the window. "See, the sun is shining already."

"Do you see a rainbow? That is a good omen," she said, putting her face close to his cheek in search of the harbinger. "Look, there it is, how beautiful."

Edward turned to face her, "Not as beautiful as the sight standing in front of me," he said with admiration.

She lowered her eyes and giggled. "Will you let me have two more mugs of coffee, to take to my driver and chaperon?"

"Stay here, and I will take it to them."

"Merci, they stopped right in front of the door."

I like that about her, concerned about the comfort of her servants.

Thibaut's and Sana's faces lit up at the sight of the hot beverage, and they quickly drank. Handing back the mugs to Eduard, Thibaut looked up at the sky, "See the rainbow? This will be a good day."

Eduard went inside, took his cloak and tri-cornered hat off the rack, and put them on. He went back to the stove where Annise was still standing. Taking her hand, he led her out of the building and helped her into the coach. He climbed in, too, and the driver called to the two horses to go.

They crossed the Seine on an ancient and ornate bridge and passed the Plaza de Republique. When Annise saw the guillotine, she shuddered and turned pale. She worried her parents might be ending their lives here in the near future. Who knew? She might even be next. Edward saw her distress and gave Sana a questioning look. She nodded her head, and he put his arms around Annise in a protective, warm way. She buried her face in his shoulder and silently wept.

"It is a good thing," Eduard said, looking at Sana, "That today there is no activity here."

The two horses and carriage wove their way through the narrow streets for another mile when they came upon a gloomy-looking building known as Temple Tower. All four stared at the four-story square building with a turret on each corner. On top was a pyramid-shaped roof.

"What do you know about that b—building?" Annise asked Eduard with a stutter.

"It was built in the thirteenth century by the Knights Templar as a dungeon. They used to have quite a walled complex here with houses and shops. The only other building remaining is that church over there."

Annise frowned. "Are there many prisoners here?"

"I don't think so. Your parents must be very important to be here."

"I cannot imagine why. They are only counts that manage a large estate. Our chateau is ornate but small. Insignificant compared to Aunt Melina's palace."

The coach pulled up to a large wooden gate in a tall stone wall. Eduard dismounted and pulled a chain that rang a bell. Soon a hole was opened in the gate, and a gruff voice inquired what they wanted.

"We are here to visit Citizens Brisson."

The peephole closed and they heard the gate being unbolted. Eduard helped Annise dismount the carriage and carried the bundle of things as both entered the garden. Several guards demanded to examine the bundle. Eduard laid it on the ground before them, and Annise untied it, to show the contents. When the guards saw the box of chocolates, their eyes lit up.

"These chocolates are for all of you," Annise said. "I thank you for taking good care of my parents." She handed the box to the grizzled old guard. "Now I know you will all share it equally."

The guard took the box and smiled. "Pierre, now take these nice people to see Citizens Brisson."

"Oui, citoyen," he said, motioning for them to follow him.

They entered through a small wooden door in one of the turrets and climbed the spiral staircase to the third floor. He unlocked another oak door and opened it. Annise saw her mother and father sitting at a table playing chess.

"*Mere, Pere!*" she shouted and ran into her mother's outstretched arms. Her father stood behind her and hugged them both. "Oh my dear parents, I have been so worried." Tears streamed down her cheeks.

"Thank you for coming," said Peter who also had tears in his eyes. "You have to tell us how everything is with you, and what is going on outside."

After a good minute, the countess looked up and saw Eduard. "Who is the young man with you, my dear?"

Annise freed herself from her parent's embrace and walked to Eduard. She took his hand. "This is Eduard Saulnier. Aunt Melina gave him permission to court me."

"We are pleased to meet you," said the count. "There must be something really special about you, to be allowed by Aunt Melina to court our dear *fille*."

"She gave me an assignment, but first let me tell you, it is a pleasure to meet both of you, alas, I wish it was under happier circumstances." He shook the count's hand, and the countess extended hers with the palm down. Eduard kissed the air above her hand and said, "*Enchante.*"

The countess looked at the bundle on the floor. "Is all of that for us?"

"*Oui*, Mama, there are clothes and underwear for both of you and other things you might like."

"We shall look at that later," said Peter. "The door is open, come we shall go and take a walk on the ramparts. The view should be excellent today."

Azelma wrapped herself in a dark blue cape with fox fur on the hem. The four people climbed the spiral staircase up to the fifth floor and the open rampart. From there they could overlook all of Paris, but, best of all, they could speak softly and not be overheard.

"Now tell me, Annise," said Azelma with an undertone of worry, "Were you able to get away with the gray cape?"

"Oui, Mere, now I know why you wanted me to take it. It is now locked in a strong box in my room at Aunt Melina's."

"I too was able to sneak out gold and silver coins in my cape. No one searched my clothes, but they certainly searched your father. What I want you to do is wear my cape out today when you go and leave yours with me. We only need a small amount of money, to pay the guard to mail our letters and do other favors."

Annise took off her blue cape and gave it to her mother. "I hope no one will notice the difference."

"As a man," said Eduard, "I would be looking at your face and not notice that the cape you came in with was dark blue with no fur on the hem, and you now have fur."

"I hope you are right," said Annise, looking concerned. Then she brightened. "You know, it just is another danger in the adventure of the day. We shall get away with the switch. We need to think positive."

"That is my daughter," said Peter, looking proud. "She has the Brisson courage."

Chapter 9

After about an hour-long visit, the guard Pierre, came onto the rampart. "Visiting time is over." Everyone left the roof and went back downstairs. At the door into the apartment, Annise gave her parents a warm hug.

"I hope to see you again soon," said Peter, shaking Eduard's hand. "It was a real privilege meeting you, young man. You take good care of our Annise."

"The privilege and pleasure are mine, your excellency."

"Citizen, just call us citizen," the count responded then whispered, "It's safer."

Before they boarded the coach, Eduard told Thibaud where to go.

While the coach was rolling into the heart of the city, Annise sighed. "It was hard seeing my parents in such a bedraggled condition. I have never seen my mother with dirty hair. And to think, she has been wearing the same dress for close to two months, day and night. The things we brought will be treasured."

"I am sure they will never again take anything for granted," Eduard said before the coach stopped.

Thibaut opened the door with alarm on his face. "Monsieur, beg your pardon, but you cannot possibly go there? We have come to the *Allee de Bourreau.* What could you possibly want here?"

"Then stay here, and Annise and I will walk."

"You cannot mean that," Thibaut said, shocked. "Sana, don't let Annise out of the carriage."

"I have my parent's permission to go with Eduard, wherever he needs to go."

She jumped out of the coach before Sana could restrain her. Eduard took her hand and hurried her toward the large gray stone house, at the end of the street.

"Now we are in deep trouble," Sana said, wiping tears from her cheeks. "I'm her chaperone, and there she goes off with the young man. Go, Thibaut, bring her back."

"I will not go into that street. See, they are already knocking on the door. It is too late. What shall we do now?"

"We better just wait for them," Sana said, resigned, "However long they take."

"That is all we can do. Fortunately, we brought some food and water and hay for the horses."

After feeding and watering the horses, Thibaut covered the animals with blankets. He climbed into the carriage, sat next to his wife, and covered both of them with a blanket. "We might as well get some rest," he said, giving his wife a hug and kiss.

"You are right," she said with a coy smile. "There is no one around. Maybe we can do more than get some rest."

"You mean—"

"*Oui,* why not?"

"Why not?"

෫ൟൟ

The fear of the servants upset Annise. "Where are you taking me? Why are they so afraid?"

"They are ignorant," Eduard said, putting his arm around her shoulder. "Do not let them frighten you. We are going to visit my friend who might be able to help us get your parents out of jail."

"Who is this powerful friend?" she said with wide eyes. "I was hoping Robespierre could help get them released. All that got them was a better prison."

"Robespierre the Incorruptible would never release them. We have to work from underneath."

They stood in front of the large leather-covered door, and Eduard pounded on it. After a while, they heard a muffled call of "I'm coming."

"You are about to meet some wonderful people. Don't let his profession frighten you."

"What is his profession?"

"The executioner."

She cringed. "You mean we are about to visit the executioner?"

"Oui, cherri, just remember, he is a very fine man with a distasteful occupation, through no fault of his own."

They heard the door being unlocked and slowly opened. In front of them stood a tall, handsome, blond-haired young man.

"Gabriel my friend, so good to see you."

"Eduard, what a pleasant surprise. And who is this beautiful young woman with you?"

"This is Annise de Brisson. Annise, meet my dear friend Gabriel Sanson."

"Enchante, mademoiselle," Gabriel said, kissing the air above her extended hand. "Come in and please go upstairs. My mother and father will be so happy to have visitors."

Eduard held Annise's trembling hand as they went up the steps. They entered the warm, well-lit apartment, and saw two people sitting at a round table, eating.

The older man spoke first. "Eduard, my young friend, how wonderful to see you again. And you bring another guest."

"Yes, this is Countess Annise de Brisson, the young lady I hope to marry. Annise, meet Olive and Henri Sanson."

Annise extended her hand, thumb up to both of them. "It is a pleasure to meet you, Madame and Monsieur Sanson."

"It is always a pleasure meeting someone other than for professional reasons," said Henri, taking her hand. "Come and have a seat at our table and break bread with us."

"Surely you two are hungry," Olive added, putting two more plates and silverware on the table. "Come and eat."

"Thank you," said Annise. "May I wash my hands somewhere?"

Olive showed her to a privy that had a brass pump for fresh water.

Once Annise sat down at the table, Olive expressed her delight. "I am so happy to have your company for supper tonight. It is so seldom we have visitors. When we do, it usually is a relative. The talk about executions gets so boring. What are you two young people doing in Paris today?"

"Yes, I can tell, Eduard," Henri said. "There is

something heavy pressing on your mind. Do you wish to talk about it now?"

Eduard took a sip of wine, put down his glass, and laid the bread on a ceramic plate. "Yes, there is a grave matter I need to discuss with you."

Annise kept her eyes on the plate in front of her. She tried to ignore the intense glances from Gabriel. She did not want to look into his beautiful corn-flower blue eyes—the eyes that looked at her as if she was the only person in the world.

Gabriel glanced at her often, while trying to hide his feelings. *She is the most beautiful girl in the world. To think, here she sits at our table. I am close enough to touch her. I did touch her, I kissed her hand. Those beautiful rosebud lips, it must be heaven to kiss them. A woman like that is way out of my reach. Me, with the cursed profession of executioner. I wish I could go somewhere where no one knows me. There are French colonies in America. Forget it, how would I ever be able to go there. Besides, some Frenchman might know me. Still, if I should go to America, I might be able to get lost in the British or German colonies.* Gabriel was so deep in thought he missed some of the conversation.

"...and the aunt gave me the challenge to get her parents out of jail before she, or even the count and countess, will give me permission to marry her. That is why we came here. Maybe you, Henri or Gabriel, have some idea how I might be able to help them."

"Do you know why your parents were arrested?" Henri asked, looking at Annise. "Was your father high in government, or an adviser to the king?"

"No, he was not. All he did was manage the large estate he owned. Our chateau is grand in a very small way. Nothing like my Aunt Melina's palace."

"The regime is after your land," Henri said. "If the count is executed as a criminal, the regime can seize the land as their own. Look what they have done to the churches, seized all their assets and printed paper notes as money. Those assignats are so easy to forge. Where are your parents imprisoned?"

"In the Tower," said Annise.

"The Tower, with the queen and the children?"

"Yes, they have the room that was occupied by the king before he—"

"Terrible day," Henri said, getting up quickly and turning his back to everyone.

He looked out of the window and wiped his eyes with a napkin. Everyone sat in silence for a few minutes.

Henri returned to the table. "They must really rate to be in the Tower."

"A few weeks ago," Annise recalled, "I met Robespierre and de Saint-Just. I asked them to help my parents. I was hoping they would just let them go, but all they did was put them into a more comfortable prison."

"And one harder to escape from," Henri added.

"We need another bottle of wine," Olive said, going

to the kitchen stove for more meat. "Gabriel, please get another bottle."

"*Oui, Mere,*" and he rose and headed for the door.

Annise paid special attention to his height and how proudly he carried his head with shoulder-length hair. *He reminds me of a fairytale prince in a book I loved as a child. Is he the prince who will rescue my parents? Will I have to marry him then?* She turned her gaze to Eduard. *He just sits there and says nothing. Is he able to help, or should I put my hope in Gabriel?*

Gabriel entered the room carrying a dusty wine bottle. "I brought one from the back of the cellar. I hope I made a good choice."

"It is getting late, and I really should be getting back," Annise said with a heavy sigh. "I hope my coach is still at the end of the street."

"Then we will drink the wine the next time we meet," Henri said. "Hopefully it will be under happy circumstances."

Olive took Annise's cloak and put it around her shoulders. She gave her a hug and touched both of the girl's cheeks with hers. "Thank you so much for coming. You are a welcome guest in our house at any time."

"*Merci* for supper. It was very good. *Au revoir, Monsieur et* Madame Sanson. Until we meet again."

"Come, my friend, Gabriel, you and I will walk mademoiselle to her carriage."

The two young men walked on either side of Annise,

and, to their delight, found the carriage with the driver and his wife waiting. Annise extended her hand first to Gabriel who took it and kissed it with his lips touching.

Eduard did the same. "I will write to you. Have a good ride back. *Bonne nuit.*"

"Bonne nuit," she said as the carriage took off into the dark.

"Come, my friend," Gabriel said. "Can you spend the night with us? We have a lot to discuss."

"It would be my pleasure. There is no one expecting me at home."

Chapter 10

The coach moved through the dimly lit streets of Paris. Annise looked at the back of her hand.

I have been kissed again. One side by Eduard and next to it by Gabriel. Who would ever think such a handsome man could have such a distasteful occupation. He looks like he could be an aristocrat, and his parents are nice and decent people. If the men did not have that horrible occupation, they could be my friends. Now Eduard is friends with them. Does that mean, if we marry, they would be my friends too?

She took a deep breath that sounded like a sigh.

"Are you well, mademoiselle?" Sana asked. "If you are cold, we can wrap into this blanket together."

"No, I feel warm. I hope you did not get too bored waiting for me."

"No, Thibaut and I had a pleasant rest. We hope your visit was good."

"Yes, they are very nice people."

"People? You mean there is a family?"

"Oui, Monsieur Sanson has a wife and son."

"I never knew that. I just thought a man like that lives alone and drinks blood."

"No, we dined off plates and drank wine."

"With silverware?"

"Certainement, and we used napkins."

"You are so brave to go there. I would never dare."

To think, just a few months ago, I too would have been afraid to go to the executioner's house. My life was so sheltered. I never saw the outside world. But what a world it is. Everything we believed in is crumbling. No more king. The churches have been raided and defaced. Those in power make fun of Christianity and want to have everyone worship pagan ideas and nature.

The coach rounded a sharp corner and Sana was pushed against Annise.

"Pardon, mademoiselle, I hope I did not hurt you."

"No, Sana, I am tough."

Yes, I am tough. I have to be. If only for Mere and Pere, who show remarkable courage. Poor Mere. I have never seen her look so neglected. Glad I could take her some soap and new clothes. Pere still looks aristocratic, in spite of the worn and dirty clothes.

"To think, now they are associating with the queen,"

Annise said out loud, without realizing it. "Is a queen without a crown still a queen?"

"I do not know. Is she?" Sana said.

"Oh, I was thinking out loud. Look, we now have moonlight."

"Yes, it is romantic going for a carriage ride by moonlight."

"You are fortunate, Sana, your husband is near. Will I ever have my love with me under a bright moon? God only knows." *Please, Heavenly Father, let my parents go free and me find happiness and love.*

The coach was traveling along the Seine River when two riders on horseback approached from the other direction. Thibaut urged the horses to go faster and reached for his pistol. The riders passed without incident before he relaxed again and slowed the horses to a comfortable trot. He stopped the coach in front of the palace and Annise hurried in. As she passed the library, her aunt called to her.

"Annise, come in here, child. Have a cup of tea and tell me all about your trip to Paris."

"Oui, Tante, I have much to tell." Annise kissed the old lady on the cheek and began her story.

c∕ɔc∕ɔ

The next day, Annise sat in her room, removing the fur from her mother's cape, along with the coins hidden underneath, and sewing the fur onto her gray cape, already heavy with gold and jewelry hidden in the lining.

The day was warm for early March, and she sat by the open window overlooking the formal garden. She saw some of the ladies living in the palace, dressed up and strolling about.

They go about their lives as if there was peace in the land and the king was still on the throne. But all is changed now. My life will never again be the same. To think, I broke bread with the executioner. And Gabriel, handsome Gabriel. If he wore fancy clothes, he could fit in with royals anywhere. More so than Eduard, who is handsome also, but not as regal looking.

"Ouch," she cried out when she pricked her finger and saw blood. "I need to concentrate on my sewing." She licked her finger and tasted the salty blood. "Do I love them both? Can a woman love more than one man at a time? Will Gabriel be the one who rescues my parents? Will that mean I need to marry him then?"

Annise shuttered as she imagined Gabriel standing on the guillotine platform and performing his job. "I could never sleep with a man who does that. Eduard, my love, please rescue my parents and become my husband."

She put her lips to the back of her hand where he had kissed her and closed her eyes, seeing his face in front of her.

When she washed her hands, she avoided running water over the back of them.

❦

Eduard sat at a table in his room in the loft. A blank piece of paper lay before him, a quill was in his hand. Next to the inkwell stood a glass of white wine. He took a sip that became a big swallow. He refilled the glass, set the bottle down, and stared at the paper. *Am I really ready to do this? It might cost me my life. If I don't get killed, I could be captured and thrown into some horrible prison and then also visit Madame Guillotine. How did I get myself into this situation?*

He dipped the quill into the ink and wrote.

Paris, March 28, 1793
Dear Mademoiselle Annise,
I begin by hoping you had a Happy Easter. Since this is Maundy Thursday, I assume you will not receive this letter until well into next week.

He took another big swallow of wine. His thoughts were racing. *I could just not mail the letter and never again plan on seeing her. Eventually, I would get her out of my mind.* He saw her face in front of him.

"Go away," he said as he closed his eyes and, in addition, saw her parents. "I can understand why she loves them like she does. Charming people, so unassuming." He took another swallow and felt the wine making him a bit lightheaded. "If all goes well, I have a beautiful loving creature to gain. If I fail, I have only my miserable life to lose. Do I find courage in the wine?"

He looked at the mostly empty bottle and continued writing.

၉၁၈၁၃

At the Chateau de Partie, the residents celebrated Easter in the traditional way. Since the holiday fell on the last day of March, the blooms of April were forced by bringing branches inside several weeks earlier, in hopes they would be open on Easter Sunday. Most blossoms were cooperating and showed themselves in full glory.

The long dining room table was decorated with apple and cherry blossoms and garnished chocolate eggs and colorful chicken eggs. Bright sunshine poured through the tall windows illumining the china and crystal. Melina Dupin sat at the middle of the table with twenty young ladies around it, dressed in their Sunday best. Melina raised her glass of wine, followed by all the guests.

"*Joyeuses Paques,*" she said, echoed by everyone in the room. "I hope France will return to normal by next Easter, and we will again hear all the church bells ringing, in praise of the Lord and the resurrection of Jesus."

"Amen," and other words of agreement sounded through the room.

Melina said a prayer off the top of her head followed

by the Lord's Prayer, recited by everyone. After the amen, the old lady rang a silver bell, and the servants came in with rack of lamb and all the trimmings. Annise thought of her parents and the times they celebrated Easter by going to church and eating a big dinner, and afterward playing games with raw eggs. It jolted her to think of the waste of good food, while others went hungry. Right then, she vowed never again to misuse good food.

Annise's mind drifted to Eduard. *I wonder what he is doing. And Gabriel, I suppose he is having dinner with his parents at the moment. Maybe Eduard is with them. Oh, I wish I knew what is going on. Poor Mere and Pere still in that dreadful tower. Why is all this happening to us? Why, Jesus and Holy Mary, why?*

ფოფ

In the middle of the week, a long-expected letter from Eduard arrived. Annise rushed into her room and read it while lying across the bed. When she finished reading, she shouted, "*Oui, oui, oui,* finally some news."

She ran down the stairs and burst into the library, where she found her aunt reading a book.

"Annise, a lady does not run in the house. Must I always repeat myself?"

"Sorry, *Tante,* but I finally have a letter from Eduard."

"Does he have good news?"

Annise opened the letter. "He begins by wishing us all a belated happy Easter. Next, he writes 'I really would like to see you. Is it possible for you to come to Paris on Thursday, April eleventh? You will find me at the newspaper *Le Pere Duchesne* starting early in the morning. To make sure you are warm, please wear your gray cloak.' He closed with 'I eagerly await seeing you again. With love,' and his name."

"What makes you so excited?"

"The fact he says to wear the gray cloak. That is a code, something important will be happening. Of course, he cannot write what it will be." Annise looked at her aunt with pleading eyes. "May I borrow a horse to ride to Paris?"

"I can't let you go by yourself. You can go in the coach with Tribaut and Sana."

"Please, Auntie, if you insist on Tribaut coming along, let him ride too." Annise took the old lady's hands and looked deep into her eyes. "It is extremely important that I go, believe me."

"Fine, take a horse and go with just Tribaut."

"Thank you, Aunt Melina, you are the best. I love you."

"Do you really think, your parents will be released?"

"I hope so, I really hope so. Please, help me pray to God, to let this have a happy ending."

"I will, my child. Now you better go upstairs and dress for dinner."

"Oui, madame." Annise pressed the letter to her chest and went to her room.

Chapter 11

On Wednesday evening, Annise took a parlor clock, that chimed every hour, into her room. After laying out her peasant attire she had come with, she carefully folded her borrowed clothes and placed them on a table.

I will wake up when the clock chimes five, she told herself as she crawled into bed. Sleep evaded her until after midnight.

When she finally went to sleep, she dreamed she was riding a horse in the streets of Paris. The streets became narrower and narrower until suddenly she was in a plaza surrounded by a mob of angry people.

They looked at her and waved their fists, shouting "Off with her head."

"Why, why do you want my head? I still need it," Annise cried out loud, waking herself up.

By the light of one candle she kept burning, she saw it only was a little after two. After a long time, she went back to sleep.

The six o'clock chimes woke Annise. Alarmed at the lateness, she jumped out of bed, used the chamber pot, and quickly washed herself with freezing water in a bowl. While dressing, she looked in the mirror and decided her hair did not need to be combed and braided again. She wrapped herself in the gray cloak and hurried down into the kitchen. The woman, who worked as cook, was getting ready to make breakfast for the residents of the castle.

"Good morning, mademoiselle, I am just now baking today's bread. All I have to give you is yesterday's."

"That is well with me. Have you seen Thibaut?"

"Yes, he already ate. He is now saddling the horses. Where are you going so early, if I may ask?"

"Just riding," Annise said with finality in her voice.

"Sorry, I was out of line. Would you like me to pack some lunch for both of you?"

"Yes, please do, and something to drink too."

While Annise ate bread and meat, the cook packed provisions.

Thibaut entered. "The horses are ready. Anytime you want to go, I am at your service."

"I am ready. Goodbye, Madame Cook." Annise took the package, handed it to the man, and they left together.

"*Adieu, mademoiselle*," said the cook, shaking her head as she watched them go out into the dark.

The horses trotted at a comfortable speed along the Seine as the first light of dawn intensified into brilliant colors. The light green leaves on the trees seemed to grow in the morning light while birds went noisily about their business of building nests and propagating the species. Annise was deep in thought and excited. *I shall be seeing Eduard again. Maybe, just maybe Gabriel will meet with us too.*

The city was just starting to wake up, as they entered Paris. While they rode through the narrow streets, Thibaut warned, "Mademoiselle, look up and watch for housewives emptying the pots into the streets."

"They still do it that way? No wonder the city stinks."

They reached *Le Pere Duchesn*e newspaper where Annise dismounted and went in. Several presses were operated by the printers. They recognized her and gave her friendly greetings. Eduard was bent over the paper and concentrating. He was unaware of her presence until she stood directly behind him and said, "Eduard."

Startled, he spun around on his stool and with delight. "Annise, you have come. How good. Are you ready for a cup of coffee?"

"I most certainly am, thank you." She took the enamel mug he handed her and looked at him with questioning eyes.

"Come, we go in the garden," he said. "There, in the gazebo, we can talk."

They went into the vine-covered gazebo, and the first thing he did was take her into his arms. "May I kiss you on your beautiful lips?"

She closed her eyes, held her chin up, and relaxed her lips. His lips eagerly made contact. His tongue gently felt her front teeth and took advantage of the space. Quickly, he let it slide deep into her mouth.

Her eyes opened wide in shock. Eduard saw her reaction and quickly pulled back. "I am sorry, *mademoiselle*, I was too forward. Please forgive me."

"It was a surprise to me. I never knew that a kiss included the tongue. Now that I know, do it again."

Eduard tightened his embrace and let his tongue slide into her mouth. She responded by doing the same to him. *To be kissed with so much passion by a man feels wonderful. I wish time would just stand still at this moment. I really think I love him.*

Eduard closed his eyes. *She's worth every risk and pain that may follow. I love her as I have never loved before. I can truly say I am willing to risk my life for her.*

"My sweet Annise, I wish we could just spend the day in each other's embrace, but I have things to tell you."

"I eagerly await your words."

"I learned, today will be your parent's trial before the Tribunal. Most people are found guilty of some drummed-up charge. We will go and sit in the gallery at the trial. After it is over, if they are found guilty, they will go back to the tower. The executions are performed in the morning, that is when they would be transported to the guillotine."

"Oh no," Annise panted, grasping her neck.

"That is when my plan will go into action. It is a good mile from the tower to La Place de la Revolution. On the way, they go through some very narrow streets. The tumbrel is pulled by one horse that is guided by one man. Two soldiers ride behind the cart on horses. There is a certain street where few people live." Eduard pulled a handkerchief out of his vest pocket and wiped his nose, taking a deep breath. "The plan is—and I have involved some friends who are royalists—we let the cart go by and raise a rope, tripping the horses. The soldiers should fall to the ground, and we club them over the head. We untie your parents and put them on the two horses. Hopefully, the animals will not be injured and lame. I will ride on a horse too, and lead them to an inn outside the city, where the landlord, who is a royalist, will let them stay."

"Where will I be while all this is going on?"

"You can be waiting for us at the inn. By the time anyone in authority knows what went on, we should be a long way off and hiding."

"I hope you are right, and all goes according to plan."

"I see apprehension in your face. I and Gabriel have gone over the plan and route, a number of times. We both feel it is the best. Now if your parents are found innocent, then we need to do nothing, and all will be good."

"What is Gabriel's role in this plot?"

"He did most of the planning."

"Will I see him?"

"Most likely not."

"Oh,"

"You sound disappointed."

"A little. I never met anyone like him. Meeting the Sansons has opened my eyes to a world I never knew. I never thought of an executioner as a real person."

"Many people feel that way, unfortunately. I could not wish for better friends, than that family."

"My servant is outside with the horses. What shall I tell him?"

"Just have him amuse himself for the day. Tell him you will not be going back until late afternoon."

"I shall need to return early in the morning," Annise looked worried. "I hope my aunt will allow me to ride off again."

"Or you could stay with the Sansons for the night. Now if your parents are found innocent, they will be released immediately and free to go back to their own chateau."

"They *are* innocent of any crime," Annise said with a jerk of the head.

"You and I know that, but if the Revolutionary Tribunal wants their land, they will be found guilty."

"I feel optimistic," said Annise with false cheerfulness. "Everything will work out well."

"We better get to the Hall of Justice," Eduard said taking her hand and walking back into the building. "Now you have to promise to sit quietly, no matter what lies you might hear said about them."

They left the building and saw Thibaut on a grassy strip of the wide street, standing with the horses. As they approached him. Eduard said, "Monsieur, we need the horses. Mademoiselle is giving you the day off. Find yourself some Parisian amusement. We will find you in the tavern over there at about five o'clock this afternoon."

"*Merci,* but I did not bring any money."

Annise reached into a leather pouch and produced some small silver coins. "Here, that should be enough for the day."

"*Merci*, that is very generous of you. Young man, you take good care of the countess."

"I will," Eduard said while helping her mount the animal. Her peasant skirt was full enough for her to ride astride. Without a backward glance, the two rode off.

They reached the Hall of Justice, as the trials for the day, were just about to begin. They found two seats in the gallery and had a good view of the courtroom.

Five judges sat behind an elevated table.

About twenty prisoners were brought in and ordered to sit on a long bench. When their names were called, they stood in front of the judges who questioned them. Count and Countess de Brisson were not among the prisoners. Eduard began to worry. All the plans were based on precise timing. An hour into the trial, the count and countess were brought into the courtroom. Peter Brisson was clean shaved and his hair cut short. Azelma wore a simple gray-green dress, and her hair was braided on top of her head like the peasants had worn for centuries. Both of them searched the faces of the people in the gallery and caught Annise's eyes. Annise raised her hand in a small wave, and both of her parents gave a slight smile and nod.

Several hours later, all the other prisoners had been tried and found guilty, except one fourteen-year-old dressmaker.

"Everyone found guilty will be executed tomorrow morning," shouted the head judge in a clear voice.

The prisoners were led out of the courtroom to be taken back to prison. They marched away with bold expressions on their faces. The only one shedding tears was the young dressmaker who was released.

"Let us get the last trial over with quickly," said the chief judge. "I'm getting hungry. What are the two prisoners accused of?"

"High treason," said the prosecutor. "Both the count

and countess who are named Citizens Brisson, have been plotting against the government and passing important documents to the enemy."

"What proof do you have?"

"I have a witness," said the prosecutor adjusting his wig. "Come forward, Citizen Gaston."

A man who had been a footman in the household stepped forward.

Annise whispered to Eduard, "That man was let go because he was caught stealing."

"Just be quiet," he whispered, reaching for her hands.

Gaston spoke in an authoritative voice. "There have been Austrian visitors to the chateau, and I have seen Citizen Brisson give them important-looking papers."

"What did Citizeness Brisson do?"

"She not only fed the enemies, honorable judge, but she also bed them." Gaston looked pleased with himself, when he heard a small gasp from the countess and some others.

Annise had a difficult time staying silent. Only the pressure of Eduard's hands held her steady.

The judges held a brief conference before the head judge rapped his gavel. "A verdict has been decided. Both citizens are guilty of high treason and will be executed, by beheading. Sentence to be carried out tomorrow, in the public square."

Another judge tapped the head judge on the shoulder and mumbled to him. Everyone in the courtroom watched intensely as the judges conferred. After several minutes, the head judge spoke.

"It has been decided that, since they are imprisoned in the tower, there is a change of plan. Instead of taking them all the way there, then transporting them again in the morning, we will just finish the job this afternoon. They will go directly from here to the guillotine. No one can say, we French are not efficient. Take the prisoners away!"

The faces of both Eduard and Annise paled. They just looked at each other with shocked expressions. Annise started shaking.

Eduard put his arms around her and whispered, "I'm so sorry, sweetheart. I tried, believe me, I really tried."

Annise just buried her face in his shoulder and cried.

Chapter 12

Suddenly, Annise stopped shaking and looked into Eduard's eyes. "I have a pistol in my garter. I will rescue them myself. Come, we must follow." She rushed outside with Eduard following a short way behind, pushing through the crowd.

Edward signaled frantically to Gabriel, who was standing by the tumbrel. Gabriel gave a slight nod.

Edward and Annise saw the count and countess being helped into the tumbrel. The executioner was tying their hands behind their backs, while two guards mounted their horses.

"The ties are loose," Gabriel whispered to the two condemned prisoners. "Keep them in place until you need to free them."

He turned to his two friends and slowly adjusted his wool stocking cap by twisting it on his head. Next, he inspected the horse's hooves at a leisurely pace. "There is a loose nail on one shoe," he called to the guards. "I have to fix it." He took a hammer from the cart and pounded on the horse's shoe. Carefully, he inspected all shoes and gave them some taps. When he saw his friends on horseback a short distance away, he told the guards, "All is well, we are ready to go."

Gabriel led the horse pulling the tumbrel slowly along the narrow Paris streets. Since this was going to be an unscheduled execution, the usual crowd of spectators was not present. Slowly they went along the River Seine.

"Can't you go any faster?" shouted one guard, following on horseback. "It will be dark soon."

"This old horse has only one speed, slow," Gabriel called back. "You will have plenty of time to make it to the tavern for a drink after we are done."

Dozens of cargo boats were tied up along the quay of the river. Gabriel raised his arm. Suddenly a young sailor, carrying a grappling hook, approached one of the soldiers and threw the hook. It grabbed him by the collar, and he was pulled off the horse.

Eduard saw his opportunity and quickly rushed toward the second soldier, grabbed him from behind, and unsaddled him.

Once the guard was on the ground, the sailor gave him a hard whack on the head with a club. The soldier had a pistol in his hand, and as he was hit, his finger pulled the trigger, hitting Gabriel in the shoulder. Meanwhile, the two prisoners slipped out of their restraints and dismounted the cart. The first soldier was slowly getting to his feet, and Peter gave him a fist in the jaw. The count felt the impact and heard a crack.

The soldier went down with blood coming out of his mouth, along with some teeth.

Annise approached the action on horseback, and the first thing she noticed was Gabriel lying on the ground and bleeding. She dismounted, tore off her white petticoat, and held it against his wound.

"Let him be," her father shouted. "He is the executioner."

"I know him. He is a friend. He was helping us."

"We have to get out of here," Eduard called. "Before the gendarmes come and arrest us all."

"Come with me quickly," the sailor, named Ezio, said in an urgent voice. "The boat is ready to go."

"Help me carry Gabriel aboard," Eduard pleaded, looking at the count. "But first we need to hide this deed."

The men quickly put the two soldiers into the tumbrel. One was moaning as he was regaining consciousness. Another whack on the head with the club by Ezio, put him back to sleep. A good slap on the hindquarters of the horses sent them all trotting off.

That accomplished, the five people gently

maneuvered Gabriel onto Ezio's boat and put him into a bunk. Ezio untied the boat, raised the sail, and the innocent-looking trading boat joined a few others catching the evening breeze heading down the river. They were several miles away from Paris by the time it was completely dark. The river traffic ceased at night, and the ships tied to pilings. It was only after the boat had stopped, that everyone aboard had the chance to breathe a sigh of relief, and get acquainted.

"Young man," Peter said, shaking Eduard's hand with both of his. "We owe our lives to you. How can we ever repay you?"

"It was my friend Gabriel, who is the real hero. He is the one who had the foresight to make alternate plans just in case. Ezio, my friend, how was it you were involved?"

"*Oui*," said the young man, "Gabriel sent me a note via a boy telling me to look out for a tumbrel coming by this afternoon and explaining what the story was."

"It certainly is my pleasure making your acquaintance, Ezio," Peter said, shaking hands.

Azelma gave him a hug.

"I hope the horses went a long way before they stopped running," Eduard said, rubbing the back of his neck, "I hope it will be some time before they launch a search party for you, Count de Brisson."

"Please, I am Citizen Brisson. No, better yet, just call me Peter."

"And my name is Azelma. I feel I am among family with all of you. Where is Annise?"

"She is below, looking after Gabriel," Eduard said. "I shall see if there is anything she needs." He went below.

"I have provisions aboard," Ezio said. "I suppose you are hungry."

"Now that you mention it," Azelma said, "I am reminded that we have had nothing since early this morning."

Ezio went below and brought back bread, meat, and beer. He ate with the older couple. Meanwhile, Eduard and Annise were below and, by the light of a whale oil lantern, tended to Gabriel's wound. She cut away his leather vest.

"Hey, that is my best vest," Gabriel complained.

"I shall sew it back together," she reassured him. "Because of the heavy leather, the ball did not go deep. Eduard, do you think you can get it?"

Eduard sat close to his friend and said nothing. He could see the lead ball nesting in the flesh. He took a knife and quickly flipped the ball out.

"Ouch," Gabriel shouted, "that hurt. But you need to hurt it some more."

"By doing what?" Annise asked.

"You need to wash the wound with vinegar."

While Eduard was searching the provision lockers for vinegar, Annise wiped Gabriel's face with cold water.

"I will forever be grateful for the actions you have

taken today." She put her face close to his and kissed him on the cheek. "If it was not for you, I would now be an orphan."

Gabriel smiled and closed his eyes. "For that kiss, it all was worth it."

Chapter 13

For the next few days, the trading boat sailed, or mostly floated, down the river. Gabriel's shoulder became infected, causing him to have a fever.

Annise sat by his bedside and wiped his brow with cold water. Azelma familiarized herself with the provisions aboard that consisted mainly of smoked sausages, onions, turnips, and the little known new food called potatoes. Combining these ingredients in a big pot and cooking them on the wood-fired stove, satisfied the crew's hunger.

Ezio was the only one aboard who knew how to sail, but Peter sat close to him at the tiller and observed how he used the sails to take advantage of the slightest breeze. By the second day out, Peter could steer the boat with skill around the bends and curves of the river. When they passed a village near the river, Ezio tied the boat to the quay or dock and brought bolts of fabrics on deck to sell. With the money received, he spent some on any provisions they could manage to buy. There was not much variety in the marketplace since it was April, and there were no new crops yet.

Eduard and Peter helped Ezio with sailing and trading, absorbing all they could learn. Day after day went by, with the big question laying on Eduard's chest. He never felt the time was right to ask the count and countess for permission to court Annise with the intention of marriage.

తుయితు

"We better just tie up to that piling," Ezio said. "With no wind and now we are beginning to get tidal effects, we'll make no progress today. We also have a job to do, and I will be needing your help, Peter and Eduard."

"What do you need to do?" Peter said.

"We need to unstep the mast."

"Why? How can we do that?" Eduard wanted to know. "How will we get to Le Havre?"

"Because there are low bridges ahead," Ezio answered in one breath. "From here, we float with the tides."

"How are we going to steer?" asked Peter.

"With those two long oars and the rudder, to an extent. We can even scull with the rudder."

"My knowledge of sailing has certainly increased during the past week, but I am sure I have much more to learn," Peter commented.

"I always say, it takes a day and a lifetime to become a good boatman," Ezio said with an alert gaze at a herd of cows. "Ah, to be a farmer and have all the food one wants just walking around."

"Are you tired of being a boatman?" Eduard asked.

"No." Ezio took a deep breath. "Not yet."

"Young man," Peter said, "I want to tell you again, we will compensate you for the passage to Le Havre. Certainly, there we can book passage to England."

"Thank you, I will need to figure the sum when we arrive in that port. I hope it still is a busy port, but I have heard rumors from other boatmen that things might have changed. Let us hope you get your ship out of France."

"I never thought," said Peter with a sigh, "That the day would come when my biggest desire is to leave France. We have lost our home and our land, but we still have our heads and our daughter. At the moment, that is the most important thing in life."

Eduard took a deep breath, placed himself in front of Peter who was sitting at the tiller and bit his lip. "Peter, there is something I want to ask you."

"We better get the mast unstepped," Ezio shouted. "Then we can call it a day."

The men jumped into action and untied the deadeyes and, following Ezio's instructions, were able to gently lay the mast on deck and lash it down. When that job was finished, Gabriel came on deck for the first time.

"Gabriel, my friend," Eduard said, reaching his hands out to him, "It is good seeing you feeling better. How does the shoulder feel?"

"Much better. It does not hurt much anymore. For the first time, I am hungry."

"As well you should be," Azelma called, bringing a pot of stew on deck, followed by Annise carrying bowls and spoons. "For the first time, we can all sit down together and dine."

"And a fine dinner it will be," said Gabriel. "It was the smell of the cooking that encouraged me to leave the bed and come on deck."

"A fine meal needs some fine liquid to accompany it," Ezio volunteered. "I shall bring out my best wine."

He went below and returned with two bottles of wine and six enamel mugs.

The warm afternoon descended into the cool of the evening. With the half moon rising above the trees, everyone just wrapped into a blanket and remained on deck, drinking good wine and conversing.

"I am happy to breathe clean fresh air again," Gabriel said. "And to be able to be among the living. Actually, it was not in the plan that I be with you. I was supposed to be tied up and laid in the tumbrel to be found by the authorities. But now that I am here, I plan to just keep going. I am happy to be away from Paris. I will miss my parents, though, and I did not take my leave from them."

"I say amen to that, young man," Azelma said. "We owe our lives to you. How can we ever repay you?"

"You can be my friends."

"We have considered you our friend all week now," Peter said, taking a sip of wine. "I am curious, how did all of you three men get acquainted?"

"Gabriel and I met in first grade," Eduard explained. "I used to go to his house to do homework."

"He defended me from all the boys in class who thought it was good sport to beat up on me just because my father had the occupation of executioner."

"I am sure your father is a fine man, seeing the son he raised," said Peter. "We are happy we did not meet him professionally."

"No one wants to meet my parents, not even socially. I tell you, I cannot think of a lonelier profession. My desire now is to get on a ship and sail to America and take up another trade."

"What would you like to do?"

"I like working with wood. I could be a carpenter or even a cabinet maker."

"That is how we met," Ezio chimed in. "My boat was hauled out, and I was trying to replace some planks. Gabriel just happened to be strolling by and saw me struggle by myself doing a two-man job. He volunteered to help me. We had the job done in a short time. I offered to pay him, but all he wanted, was to sit with me and enjoy some wine. We became friends over two glasses of wine." Ezio raised his mug. "*Pour votre sante et amitie.*"

Everyone raised their mugs too and echoed, "To your health and friendship."

"How did you become a boatman?" Annise wanted to know.

"I was born one. My mother and father traded up and down the river, and she bore me aboard this boat. I grew up helping them work. My schooling is limited, but I am very good with figures."

"I assume your dear parents are deceased then," Azelma commented.

"No, they wanted to retire and move ashore. I bought the boat from them, and with the money, they could buy a cottage. They live not very far from Le Havre."

"Maybe you can visit them when we are there," Annise said.

"I would like to do that."

Eduard sat across the table from Annise, who sat between her parents. *Here she is, so close, yet so far away. She looks so pale and vulnerable by the light of the moon. I wish I could just take her into my arms and kiss her like I did in the gazebo.* He felt some stirring in his crotch. *Down boy, behave yourself. This is not the time or place.*

"Eduard," said Peter, "this afternoon you had a question for me. What do you want to know?"

"Madame and Monsieur—"

"Using those terms," Gabriel said, "got some people condemned. Please get used to always saying Citizen. Sorry to interrupt you."

"Good reminder," Eduard said. "I caught myself using those terms in the city. I suppose I am fortunate not to have said it to the wrong people."

"What was your question for me?"

"It is a question for both of you, Count and Countess," he said, whispering the noble title. "Madame Dupin gave me an assignment or challenge, you might call it. If I could complete it to success, she or you would give me permission to court Annise, with the intention of marriage."

Peter leaned forward and inquired, "What was the assignment?"

"To get you and your wife out of jail, any way I could. The fact that we are all here proves my challenge was successful. Now, I ask for your blessings to my courting your daughter."

Peter and Azelma leaned back against the wooden railing, and each one let out their breaths. They both looked at Annise and said nothing for a long minute. Annise looked at Eduard with hope and apprehension. Finally, Peter spoke.

"Eduard, you are a very brave young man, and we

are honored to know you. All three of us are eternally grateful for what you and your two friends have done. But as far as marrying our daughter," Peter let out a sigh, "There is a complication."

Chapter 14

"C omplication?" Eduard said with a stiffening posture. He felt as if his heart had dropped out of his body and was replaced by a big boulder. "What might that be? Is it because I am just a commoner and have no noble title?"

"No, the fact that you have no title does not matter to us. Titles can be dangerous nowadays," Peter said, clutching his neck. "It is this—Annise was promised to another man."

"I was?" Annise shouted in a high-pitched voice. She looked thoughtful. "Oh yes, now I remember. But they left the country a year ago. You mean that engagement is still valid?" She looked intensely at Eduard. "It is the son of the adjoining estate to our property. At least, what used to be our property. He is a young marquis." Tears came to her eyes. "*Mere, Pere,* I love Eduard. He risked his life, along with his friends' lives for you. You will just have to give your blessings for us to get married."

"It is not that simple, my cherri," Peter said, putting his arm around her shoulders. "The Marquis de Castellane, Lukas's father, and I had a gentleman's agreement that our children were to wed when both of you turn eighteen. Just because they fled to England does not void the contract. I understand they live in a palace near Southampton. They will be eager and happy to give us shelter, especially when our children are wed."

"*Mere, Pere*, I like Lukas, but I love Eduard," Annise pleaded with tears running down her cheeks. "Please find a way to get out of this agreement."

"I am a gentleman, and to us, our word is binding. I am sorry my love, and Eduard, but I am not at liberty to give you two my blessings."

"In ten days, I will have my eighteenth birthday. Please, Papa, think of a way for this engagement to become invalid."

"I can think of a way," Azelma said. "But I will not mention it."

Peter gave her a puzzled look then realized what she was thinking. "It certainly would not be something a lady would tell her daughter."

Gabriel moaned softly. "I have been sitting too long now. I need to get into my bunk." He rose and started down the ladder, "*Bonne nuit*, everyone. I enjoyed the evening. Cheer up, Eduard and Annise. You two are meant for each other, and all will be well."

"I hope so, Gabriel," Annise said. "Goodnight and sleep well,"

"It has been a long day," said Peter, "Time for us to get our rest too. Come Azelma and Annise."

Azelma followed her husband below, but Annise lingered on deck and waited for Ezio to go below. Once alone, she sat down next to Eduard and put her arms around him.

"Kiss me, please kiss me like you have never kissed me before."

Eduard wrapped his arms around her body, put his lips to hers, and kissed her, allowing his tongue to feel as far as it could reach. She reacted by breathing hard, and her hips started to gyrate. *I could just take her now. She would let me deflower her and become a ruined woman. I can just see Peter catching us in the act, tie me to the anchor, and throw me overboard.* He withdrew his tongue and ended the kiss.

"Again, please," she said, putting her lips on his and allowing her tongue to search in his mouth. When they once again parted, she said, "I need to say goodnight, my love. I shall see you in the morning."

She went below while Eduard remained on deck and finished all the wine.

Chapter 15

At the first light of dawn, Ezio found Eduard lying on deck wrapped in a blanket. His head was leaning over the side, and the rancid odor of puke was present. Ezio took a long pee overboard, brushed back loose strands of hair, and tied them into the long, brown braid hanging down his back. He gently nudged Eduard with his foot.

"Time to get up, Eduard. Tide's going out, we need to get underway."

Eduard moaned. "Just let me be. I shall just lie here and die."

"You can't die here, you are in my way. Get up and find a better place to expire."

"Just throw me overboard." He sat up and put his

hand on his forehead. "Ouch, that hurts. The wine tasted good going down. Now I have demons in my head, trying to get out."

"It would do no good throwing you overboard. You told me you can swim. In that case, you might as well decide to live and help me get the boat to Le Havre."

"Why live? All my hopes and plans and dreams for naught. I love that girl and want to marry her. Now I find out she is promised to another."

"But because of you, her parents live. Your actions saved their lives."

"Actually, I only was the one who started it, Gabriel is the real hero. I cannot even claim to be a hero. I am a total failure. There is only one thing I am sure of," Edward said rising.

"What is that?"

"I have to pee, that is the only thing I know for sure." He stood at the stern of the boat and let it flow into the Seine.

Gabriel stepped on deck and, after a greeting, also took his place at the stern and contributed to the volume of the river.

"Look," Gabriel said, "I can pee farther than you."

The other two men laughed. "I am so glad you still have your sense of humor, Gabriel," Ezio said. "We need to cheer up our friend here, but you just made him laugh. There is hope he will remain among the living."

Next, Peter stepped on deck with a bucket, said

bonjour, and threw the contents overboard. "Azelma is rising, but Annise is not well."

"What is the matter?" Eduard said, looking grieved.

"It is that time of the month for her."

"Will you allow me to visit with her?"

"Wait until Azelma finishes dressing herself."

"I am going forward to untie the boat," Ezio said. "The current is speedy today. I will need everyone's help when we approach that stone bridge ahead." He pointed to an arched bridge. "We aim for the center span."

The four men reached for oars and boat-hooks and slid under the bridge, without rubbing sides.

"Well done, men," Ezio said. "You are the best crew I ever had."

"Do you have a crew normally?" Gabriel inquired.

"Yes, a young boy, but he was visiting his parents when we departed Paris in such a hurry."

"How will you get the boat back upstream?" Peter said.

"Hopefully I can find a boat hand in Le Havre."

"One good thing," Gabriel said. "You were able to sell all your fabrics along the way. I would be happy to help you take the boat back, but I hope to find a ship for America. I know my parents are worried about me. I wrote them a letter, and I hope to mail it in the next town where we stop."

Azelma showed herself at the hatch. "*Bonjour monsieur*, I have cooked some oatmeal and found honey in the back of a locker."

"Good," said Ezio, "I am hungry. Are you too, Eduard?"

"I might be able to eat a little. But first, I would like to visit with Annise."

"Do that, she is awake. But first, help me give out the food." She handed him bowls of oatmeal with a dab of honey on top, and he passed it to the other men.

"I might eat after my visit."

"Take her some hot chamomile tea," said Azelma. "That might make her feel better."

Annise was in her bunk in a fetal position facing the wooden bulkhead.

"Annise," Eduard said softly.

"Go away, *Pere*. Leave me alone."

"Annise," he said louder, "It's Eduard."

She turned toward him and reached out. "Eduard, my love."

He set the mug of hot tea down and rushed into her embrace. "Oh, my dear Annise. What are we going to do? I do not want to go through life without you by my side. The thought of being Lukas's wife repulses me, now that I know you. You and I simply must get married. Maybe we can run off together and go where no one knows us." She rubbed her stomach, "Owe, I have never had so much pain with the curse before."

"Here, drink this tea, your mother says it might help."

"But it will not help the pain in my heart."

"At the moment, you are far away from the young marquis and—"

"That effeminate marquis,"

"And we are close together."

"Not close enough."

"Things may just work out in our favor, and we can spend our lives together."

Before Annise could reply, Peter drew the curtain aside. "Eduard, you are needed on deck."

He went outside, and Gabriel and Ezio were preparing to dock at a fair-sized village. Edward saw he was not really needed. *I see the Brissons want to make sure that I have no opportunity to get intimate with Annise. Maybe that should be my next challenge.*

While the boat was tied to the dock of the village, the count and two women remained below deck, while the three young men walked to the market.

"I will be so glad when summer comes again," said Gabriel as they approached the area around the church where the market was. "I yearn to eat green vegetables again."

"Oui," Ezio chimed in. "And nice red tomatoes."

"Just thinking of tomatoes makes my mouth water," said Eduard. "Not to mention crisp green cucumbers."

"Thank the provinces for pickled cucumbers at least," said Gabriel, who saw a young vendor and was increasing his stride. "Let us buy something from that fair lass, whatever she is selling."

The mademoiselle looked up and smiled at the three strangers. "Turnips and carrots I have today. How much would you like?"

"Give us two kilos of each. Would you have potatoes?" said Ezio.

"Oui, what animals do you feed with them?"

"No animals, just us."

"You eat potatoes?" she said with big eyes. "I was told they are poison for people."

"Whoever told you that," said Gabriel, "was either lying or ignorant. I can assure you, young lady, potatoes do no harm."

"How do you prepare them?"

"First we cook them in water, peel them, put butter on, and eat it like it was bread. You should try it."

"Merci for the suggestion. I will do that."

"We need butter also," Eduard added.

"Go across the plaza and buy some from the lady in the brown skirt. She has good cheeses too."

Ezio and Eduard started walking off, but Gabriel lingered. "Is there still mail service in town?"

"Yes," she said, pointing toward the tavern. "The innkeeper is also our postmaster."

"Merci, Citizen, it was my pleasure doing business with you."

"Take good care of yourself," she said, watching him with longing eyes as he walked away.

When Gabriel entered the tavern, the innkeeper right

away noticed the tall stranger and asked what he needed.

"A glass of wine might taste good right now," said Gabriel. A minute later, he had his wish. "They tell me, you are the postmaster here."

"You heard correct."

"How is the mail service these days?"

"To tell you the truth, the service is not as good as it used to be, but one can manage to get a letter to the proper person eventually."

"I have a letter to go to Paris."

The innkeeper mentioned the price.

"That is a lot more expensive than it used to be."

"So is the price of food and wine," said the man behind the counter. "If this keeps up, they will charge us for the French air we breathe."

"Do not give those in power any ideas," said Gabriel with a chuckle. He paid for the postage and wine and returned to the boat.

☙❧

It was afternoon as the boat slowly floated downstream. Eduard sat at the tiller with Annise beside him. The count and countess sat near the bow, enjoying the passing scenery. Gabriel and Ezio were below stowing their recent purchases of provisions. Annise put her face close to Eduard's and closed her eyes. He looked at her parents and saw them looking the other way.

Eduard's lips connected with Annise's. She opened her eyes as the boat passed a road that intercepted the road along the river. In the distance, she saw a troop of marching soldiers.

"Look," she said, pointing a shaking arm. "Do you think they are looking for us?"

"Most likely they are looking for men to draft. We three men qualify for the French army."

Peter and Azelma hurried to go below, followed by Annise.

"We need to look like old men. Ezio, where is the flour?" Gabriel asked.

Ezio produced a canister of flour, and the three young men combed the powder into their hair.

"I will put my braid inside my shirt and sit like I have a humpback," said Ezio. "None of us want to go into any stinking French army."

For several hours, the boat, with the three *old* men aboard, drifted at marching speed. They could see the envious glances the soldiers gave them. By late afternoon, the troops turned away from the river road. At dusk, those aboard the boat saw Le Havre ahead.

Chapter 16

Ezio managed to row the boat, with the help of the three men aboard, into the harbor after dark. They expected to find a busy port with many ships. Instead, the only docked ship was a French naval vessel.

"I cannot believe this," said Ezio. "Last year when I was here, this was a busy port with ships from Spain and England and even some from the Americas. Now, this looks like a ghost harbor."

Peter sighed. "I was expecting to be able to buy passage to England on a trader. Now that does not look possible. What are we going to do?"

Azelma, who was sitting next to her husband, started crying. "First the mob breaking into our chateau then that horrible little cell in Paris. Our condition improved a bit in the tower, but then the horror of going to the guillotine. We tolerated the discomfort of this boat, hoping to get passage to England and meet up with Marquis and Marquise de Castellane. Now, here we are, afraid to go on land. What are we going to do?"

"If I did not have my hands on an oar, I would give you a big hug and dry your tears," Peter said. "Now here is where we have to show courage and backbone and not cry."

"What options do we have, Father?" Annise asked, patting her mother's shoulder.

"Ezio," Peter said, "why don't we just take this boat and sail to England?"

"Sir, this is a riverboat. In my opinion, she is not fit for the English Channel."

"How far is it across?" Eduard asked.

"Over a hundred miles," Ezio said.

"That far?" Gabriel said. "But if we go ashore, I fear being conscripted into the army, along with you my friends. Surely, Citizens Brisson would be arrested. I am willing to risk sailing across. The wind is gentle, and the sea is calm. What is there to stop us?"

"Over a hundred miles of open water and swift currents," Ezio said. "We have no idea where we can end up."

"We have a long English coast to aim for," Peter said. "Ezio, how about I buy the boat from you? Did you not tell me you have parents living nearby? With the money, you can buy another boat, or whatever you wish."

"Count Peter, that offer sounds to my liking. For five pieces of gold, you can buy the boat and everything that is aboard. Eduard and Gabriel had the opportunity to learn to sail." He studied the coastline by the light of the full moon. "Let us take the boat over there to that empty beach, and we shall step the mast and conclude the business."

By the time day dawned in gray light, the mast was stepped and the sails ready to hoist. When the tide floated the boat off the sand, the men raised the sails and took off.

Ezio stood on shore and watched until the boat became a small speck on the horizon. He patted the leather pouch which held the gold coins, among smaller silver money, and walked toward the city. *I do not feel guilty charging the count way too much for the boat. After all, I risked my life to save both of them. Who knows, if anyone will ever see any of them again. Any money they have could end up at the bottom of the English Channel. I hope they make it across, I really hope so. But in that boat, their fate is in the hands of God.*

Ezio strolled along the street as the city was waking up. At a livery stable, he bought a horse and saddle and took off in a gallop toward his parent's house.

ርሳርሳ

The little sloop seemed happy, sailing in the late April sunshine on a calm sea. Eduard had his hand on the tiler and Annise sat next to him keeping her eyes on the red sails. A gentle wind kept them filled, with the boat at a slight heel.

The continent receded into the distance until they saw nothing but water.

"How do you know where we are going?" Annise asked.

"See, this compass needle points north, and we are going where it points."

"That is so clever. If we were going south, would it point that way then?"

Eduard chuckled. "No, it always points north."

Peter, who was sitting nearby, remarked, "I do not like to see those heavy dark clouds in the west. They are sagging into the sea and coming closer."

Azelma stepped onto deck with a basket on her arm. "I made sandwiches for supper. Here, eat," she said, handing them out. "Is this wind getting stronger or is it my imagination?"

"Unfortunately it is not your imagination," said Peter as a gust of wind filled the sails and lay the boat at a steep angle. "Hold on!" he shouted as a wave washed partly on deck.

Gabriel stepped out with a bucket of water and threw

it overboard. "The boat is taking on a lot of water. I need help with bailing."

"First we need to lower the mainsail," Eduard shouted. "Annise, take the tiller and point the boat into the wind."

The men ran on the top deck, preparing to lower the sail and tie it up while Annise tried to control the tiller.

"Mama, come help me! We need to put the tiller to the opposite side of where we want to go."

Azelma sat on the other side of the tiller. With Annise pushing and the countess pulling on the rounded plank of hardwood, they managed to ease the wind out of the sails for the men to lower the mainsail and secure it to the boom. The boat sailed under the small jib.

"Well done," praised Eduard as he again took hold of the steering while the others went below, filling containers with water, and throwing them overboard. He could see the hull going deeper underwater. By the fading light of day, he saw a ship on the horizon. "A ship! I see a ship! How does it look below?"

"The water is gaining on us," Gabriel called. "We are sinking."

"We need to make a fire," Eduard said, "To signal our distress."

"Lord, help us," Azelma pleaded while throwing a pot-full of water overboard. "Soon it will be dark, and we are in deep peril. Please send your angels to save us."

"If that is a French ship, we are doomed," Peter said.

"I would rather take my chances on this boat."

"Sir," Eduard argued. "It is only a matter of time, and this boat will sink."

Annise gasped. "Father, we just have to take that chance. That ship might be able to save our lives."

"Yes, Peter," Azelma added. "The thought of drowning does not appeal to me. This is an answer to my prayers. Those are God's angels come to help us." She went below and gathered an arm full of firewood.

Annise brought the lit hanging oil lamp on deck and made a fire in a large frying pan. While everyone was bailing as fast as they could, Eduard worked the tiller, while watching the ship approach.

"Are you in trouble?" a voice called across the water in English.

Azelma, who was proficient in that language, shouted back, "Yes, we are sinking!"

"Extinguish the fire, and we will pull alongside!" shouted a loud baritone voice. "Throw us some lines."

Azelma quickly spoke the commands in French. Everyone jumped into action. Gabriel grabbed the pan with fire and threw it overboard. Eduard went to the bow with a line, and Peter did the same at the stern. When the ship was close, both men tossed the lines to willing hands who held them.

A rope ladder was lowered. Azelma pulled her skirt between her legs, secured the hem in her belt, and climbed up the ladder, closely followed by her daughter.

Annise wore the cloak with money and jewels, along with some Peter carried in his clothes. Peter was next to catch hold of the ladder and climbed up with Eduard right behind him. Before Gabriel could catch the ladder, the boat sank, pulling Gabriel under.

All onlookers gasped seeing him disappear. A few seconds later his head broke surface. He swam toward the ladder and caught a hold of it. Again reunited, the five shipwrecked sailors hugged each other before they looked around and wondered where they had landed.

They studied the faces of the crew staring at them. Some men were black, but most were white. The youngest looked to be about twelve with light blond hair. Most men had beards, a few were clean shaven.

They all wore an assortment of clothing, none wore uniforms. A young man with a beard and no mustache, wearing a black business suit, stepped forward and spoke English in the baritone voice that echoed in the chests of all who heard him.

"What the hell were you people doing out here in that little riverboat? Don't you have any respect for the English Channel?"

Azelma stepped forward. "We are French aristocrats, escaping from the regime, and are grateful for you coming to our rescue. We are trying to get to England. If you can take us there, we will be glad to pay you. I assume you fine people are British merchants."

"You assume wrong, little lady. We are American

privateers. The only reason we are in this cursed English Channel is because we were blown off-course. There is no way we are going anywhere near that damned England. Are you the only one in your group who speaks English?"

"I think so. Everyone speaks French." She turned to the group and asked, "Does anyone speak another language?"

"I speak some English and a little German," said Eduard in English.

"We have Heinz and Sepp who speak German. There are Remi and Sami who speak French. I am Captain Young, and my language is only English."

"Thank you again for saving us from drowning," said Azelma. "Now if you allow us to introduce ourselves, she reached for Peter. "This is my husband, Count Peter de Brisson, and our daughter, Annise. I am Azelma, and these are our dear friends, Eduard Saulnier and Gabriel Sanson."

"On this ship, we use only first names, other than for myself, of course," said the young captain with an air of superiority. "The only accommodation I can offer you is the sail locker. You may dine with me in the officer's mess."

"Could you tell us where you are taking your vessel?" Azelma asked while the others wondered what was said. Gabriel, who was all wet started to shiver.

"Remi," commanded the captain, "Take that young

man into the galley and let him warm up with a hot drink and find him something to wear." Turning to the refugees, he said, "All of you can go down into the galley and warm up. I have to tend to the ship and get the hell out of this damned channel." The captain turned his back and shouted to the crew," Lower the fore t'gar'ns!"

A number of men sprang into action.

Chapter 17

After a little snack of hard tack with butter washed down with hot tea, Remi led the five refugees through the large open space filled with hammocks. Many of them were occupied by sleeping sailors. Ten cannons stood along each side of the hull. The hatches in front of the barrels were closed and wooden crates containing cannonballs stood next to each weapon. Peter, Eduard, and Gabriel had to walk stooped over, the two women could just stand upright below the deck beams. Remi was a talkative sailor and proud of his French heritage.

"My parents brought me to America when I was a little *bebe.* We settled in a French Colony in South Carolina where I grew up. I always liked the ocean and wanted to work on a ship. I was lucky enough to get hired on this corvette. It was not until our first battle, I learned this is a privateer."

"What is the difference between a pirate and a privateer? Peter asked.

"We have a Letter of Marque from George Washington. We go only after ships that are enemies of the United States. Pirates go after all ships, and when they get caught, they are hanged. If we get caught, we become prisoners of war."

"Aren't you afraid?" said Azelma "Battles are so dangerous."

"There are hazards, but the pay is really good," said the young man, while taking a hanging oil lantern off a hook and guiding his countrymen into the clean sail locker. "Captain Young is a good seaman and, with our twenty guns and maneuverability, we make quick work of merchant ships. We do not kill the crew, unless we have to."

The refugees looked around at the piles of white cotton sails.

"This is the best the captain has to offer you. We have blankets for all of you, and you can see daylight through the hatch. Be careful opening it, we do not want the sails to get wet."

"Thank you with all our hearts," said Peter. "All of us are grateful. If it was not for your ship coming along, we would all be on the bottom of the channel now. We bid you *bonne nuit.*"

"*Bonne nuit,*" said Remi, leaving the lamp hanging on a hook. "Once you have settled in, please extinguish the light."

The refugees found some fairly flat surfaces and stretched out. Azelma lay next to her daughter and Peter on the other side of her. Next lay Gabriel and beyond him was Eduard. Peter blew out the lantern, and intermittently the moonlight of the almost full moon lit the room. When Annise heard her mother's slow deep breathing, she slipped away from her and crawled next to Eduard. When he felt movement next to himself, he whispered, "Is that you, Annise?"

"Yes," she responded. "Please hold me."

He obliged. She put her mouth close to his ear. "What date is it tomorrow?"

"I believe the twenty-eight, why?"

"If tomorrow is Sunday, it will be my birthday. I will turn eighteen. Do you know what that means?"

"You are old enough to get married."

"And old enough to…you know. I want you to take me."

"But we need to wait until after midnight," Eduard whispered as softly as he could.

"How will we know the time?"

"I do not know. In the meantime, I shall kiss you."

The kisses did not last long. Both of them fell asleep in each other's arms.

At the first light of day, Annise crawled back and lay next to her mother as if she had been there all night.

A short time later, Peter woke up and left the sail locker. He passed the galley and saw the cook. "*Bonjour.*"

"*Bonjour, monsieur, comment allez-vous?*"

"You speak French. The captain did not mention the cook is French too."

"The cook is often forgotten until it is time to eat. *Oui, monsieur,* I too come from France. Emigrated with my parents when I was a child. But that is a story by itself," said the cook, starting to knead the dough.

"I would be interested in hearing your story when you have time."

"I can talk and work, not like some people. Have you ever noticed there are people who stop working to talk?"

"Oh, yes," said Peter with a chuckle. "I had a tailor like that. Could never talk to him during a fitting, if I did not want to stand all day in a half-made garment. Where in America are your parents?"

"They are in a city called New York. My father had to leave France quickly because the police were after him."

"Oh?" said Peter with raised eyebrows. "Why?"

"My father is a furniture maker and did some fine pieces for the nobility. That damned nobility are notorious poor payers, at least some of them. Tradesmen have to eat too, you know."

"Of that I am aware."

"There was this count near Marseillaise who did not pay. My father got desperate, and the next time he delivered an item, he knocked the old man on the head and simply took the money he was owed. He even took some extra, called it interest for the time it was owed."

"I can understand that."

"That same day, we boarded a ship and sailed to America. Best decision my parents ever made. Breakfast will be served in an hour."

"I have no timepiece. How will I know when an hour is up?"

"You will need to listen to the ship's bell. Someone rings that every half hour. When you hear eight bells, go to the captain's table," the cook said while he formed the dough into loaves.

"I enjoyed talking with you. Hope we can do it again soon. *Au revoir.*"

"Always good to have company. I do not have much opportunity to speak French anymore."

Peter went on deck and observed the sunrise. *Thank you, Lord, for allowing me to see another day. Last night I thought by now I would be wherever one goes when one dies. Maybe there is a heaven or maybe there is nothing, like the regime tries to tell us. I believe you exist, and to me that is all that matters.*

A sailor walked by and wished Peter a good morning. Peter wanted to ask him a question, but remembered the language barrier. He just returned the greeting in French. Standing at the railing, he looked at the water beneath him. *We came really close to being fish food.* He looked up and saw the rest of his party coming on deck.

Azelma asked a sailor to bring a bucket of water aboard for them to wash in.

The sailor took a small canvas bucket on a rope and brought up sea water. The five people gathered around it and washed their faces and hands, then they heard seven chimes on the bell.

"In half an hour, we go for breakfast," Peter said.

At eight bells, the refugees seated themselves at the table with the captain, first mate, and the ship's doctor. A steward brought in a basket of still warm rolls, along with some meat and jam. The beverage was black coffee.

The steward served the captain first, then the guests. He saw the surprised expression on Azelma's face. He simply said, "On a ship, the captain always gets served first."

Azelma nodded and, with a smile, told the others. She could hardly eat since she was the interpreter, and, as usual, Peter was full of questions.

"Where are we now?" he wanted to know.

"Thanks to the current and the wind letting up, we made it to the western end of the English Channel," said

Captain Young. "I want to inform you, that at two bells this morning we shall gather on deck for religious service."

"Is that a daily event?" Azelma asked for everyone.

"No, only on Sunday."

Annise gave her parents a questioning look. *It does not look like they remember today is my birthday. A week ago we talked about that the Sunday coming I will be eighteen, and by now it is forgotten.* She glanced toward Eduard who sat across the table from her.

He smiled and mouthed, "*Joyeux Anniversaure, je t'aime.*"

"I love you too," she mouthed back, unnoticed by the others.

"Where do you plan to go from here?" was the question everyone wanted to know the answer to.

"We are looking for British naval vessels. Those bastards, pardon my strong words, impress American seamen into their navy. Take them right off our ships. It is my God-given duty to rescue as many of them as I can."

As the countess was telling everyone, shocked expressions came to their faces.

"Does that mean we will get into a real sea battle?" Eduard said in mostly English.

"It is likely," responded the captain.

"What about the women?" Peter wanted to know.

"The safest place on the ship is my cabin in the stern.

If it comes to a battle, all of you need to remain there."

"If there will be a battle," Eduard said bravely, "I would like to help fight."

"That I forbid. Untrained men would only get in the way and endanger others. All of you would need to remain below."

Since the weather was warm and calm, the windows of the mess hall were open. Suddenly a shout was heard, "Sail ho!"

The captain and mate jumped up and ran out.

Chapter 18

A short time later the steward entered and closed the windows. "I am sorry to say, but the captain informed me we will engage in battle. You are to come with me into his quarters. We feel it is the safest place on the ship."

"Will we ever be safe again?" Azelma asked no one in particular. She wrung her hands on her skirt and started trembling. Peter embraced her from the side as they followed the steward down the passage.

Eduard hugged Annise and whispered, "We will survive this too."

She let him hold her without feeling guilty.

Gabriel lingered behind, at first, then hurried off in the opposite direction. He emerged on deck and saw activity that reminded him of watching ants when he disturbed their dirt mount as a child. Sailors pushed rolled up hammocks against the sides of the deck against the railing. Others climbed up into the rigging to lower all the sails the ship carried. Gabriel went below again and watched the crew load the cannons. Some were loaded with one ball while others received double balls with either a bar or chain between them. Gabriel saw Sami and asked, "What are the double cannon balls for?"

"They are good to take down the rigging," he said, while adding gunpowder.

Gabriel followed the French sailor. "What can I do to help?"

"Stay out of the way," Sami said.

Gabriel went back on deck and saw the distance between the ships had shortened. The other ship was huge in comparison. The captain stood on the poop deck and held a telescope to his eye. From aloft the cry of "SAIL HO" was heard. Up in the crow's nest, the sailor was pointing beyond the ship. The captain kept looking through the telescope for a good minute while everyone was frozen, ready to spring into action.

The captain shouted a command and the crew burst into motion. Two helmsmen turned the wheel, the sails were adjusted, and the ship pulled away from the approaching vessels. When the ships were almost out of sight, everyone breathed a sigh of relief and started to relax. Gabriel found Sami and spoke with him.

"We were going to take on one British naval vessel," Sami explained proudly, "But there is no way we could conquer two of them. One of those ships carries sixty guns, to our twenty."

"I noticed that," said Gabriel. "Yet we were going to take them on?"

"The reason we can do that is because we can outmaneuver them and we are speedier. It is like a dog going after a bear."

"But at times, the bear makes quick work of the dog."

"That is the chance we take. Life is dangerous. No one gets out of it alive."

"Yes, that I well know."

"What is your profession?"

"I am a carpenter and cabinet maker."

"How did you end up on the riverboat?"

"I helped rescue the count and countess from the guillotine."

Another sailor came along and spoke to Sami in English.

"It is my turn to man the bilge pump," Sami said and went below.

Gabriel went back to the captain's quarters and explained what had transpired to the waiting group.

"Thank God," Azelma responded. "The last thing in the world I wanted was to be in a sea battle. Peter, please do something to get us off this ship."

"I hope we can have a quiet dinner with the captain and talk with him," Peter said with a sigh. "I have no desire to spend the rest of my life on a ship either."

"Now the danger is over," said Annise. "May I remind you, my dear parents, what we can celebrate?"

Both looked at their daughter with a questioning expression. Azelma's face lit up in a big smile. "It is your birthday today." She reached for her daughter and gave her a big hug. "All our best wishes for a very happy and a great year to follow."

"It will be if you allow me to wed Eduard," she said with a wavering smile.

"We explained to you a week or more ago that, at the moment, we cannot give our blessings," Peter explained. "I promise you this, when we get on land, I shall write a letter to his father and ask for a release from the contract." He reached toward his daughter to give her a hug. "That is all I can promise you."

"And suppose the old marquis does not agree, will I be forced to marry Lukas? I will kill myself first."

Azelma's face lost all pinkness. "My dear child, do not speak like that. Do you want to go to hell for all eternity?"

"Marrying Lukas could be hell on earth. There might not even be another hell."

Azelma collapsed into a chair, reached for a sheet of paper, and fanned herself. "I think that child will make me faint."

"I am going on deck," said Annise. "Come, Eduard, walk with me."

To her surprise, her parents did not try to stop her. Eduard shrugged his shoulders and followed her with Gabriel close behind.

"Make sure, she does nothing foolish," Peter called after Eduard. He turned to his wife, "You and I need to get some fresh air too. Come on deck with me."

"Oh, what I would give for a clean dress right now. I hate to be seen in this dirty and torn dress, and all that salt crusted on the skirt."

"When we get ashore you can buy the finest dresses available. Come on deck with me, I want to walk with my beautiful wife."

"Oh, Peter, you are such a flatterer. *Je t'aime*."

"And I always love you."

When they went on deck, the ship sailed at a good speed out of sight of land and other vessels. The captain stood on a crate reading from the bible while all the men sat on the deck listening. In conclusion, they sang a hymn all knew. When the service was finished, the captain and first mate took an instrument and pointed it at the sun.

"What are they doing?" said Azelma.

"Navigating by measuring the angle of the sun. How they find out where they are is a mystery to me. There are so many things I want to ask the captain during dinner."

"You make it almost impossible for me to eat. You should have learned English too."

"You are right, my dear. I never saw any reason in the past, since French is the court language all over Europe. Start teaching me right now." He swept his arm indicating the ship. "What is this called?"

"A boat or ship."

"And what do you call that young couple over there?"

"Many names, your daughter, your future son-in-law, hopefully, a hero, a couple,"

"I see Gabriel in deep conversation with Sami and Remi. I wonder what they are discussing."

"America, I would wager. They are telling him what it is like. Come, Peter, let us sit over there on the ropes and leave the young people in peace. It is lovely being in the sunshine."

കൃക

That evening at the dinner table, the captain informed everyone that the ship needed to be dry docked.

"We have more of a leak than normal," explained Captain Young. "We will take her to Ireland."

"Ireland?" said Azelma with widening eyes. "What about us?"

"You will be free to leave the ship," the captain said with a hopeful tone. "We do not know how long she will be in the shipyard, that can be a few weeks."

By the time Azelma finished translating, Peter had

his questions ready. "Are you not afraid the English will capture you?"

"The Irish are no friends of the English. It goes back to the days of the English ruling the country with an iron hand. The Irish are our friends," said the captain, taking a big sip of red wine. "I plan to take the ship up the Suir River a way. Everybody pray for favorable wind."

"What is the best way to get to England?" Azelma asked.

"You can get a boat to take you to Wales and from there travel to wherever you want to go. Why is it you want to go to England?"

"We have friends there and our daughter, Annise," the countess explained, motioning toward her sitting next to Eduard, "Is engaged to marry a French marquis."

"You mean those two young people are not married?" the captain looked surprised. "They look like they are in love."

Azelma was silent.

"What did he say, *Mere*?" Annise asked.

"He thought you and Edward were married."

"I wish we were," Annise said, reaching for Eduard's hand. *I think my parents forgot my birthday again.*

Edward raised his wine glass and in halting English he said, "I propose a toast to Annise. Today, she turns eighteen. *Joyeux* birthday, my love."

Everyone else raised their glasses and wished her a memorable birthday."

"Yes, a memorable day it is and always will be," responded the girl in French. "And Eduard and I will be married soon."

The steward entered with a cake and one lit candle. "The cook and crew wish you a joyful birthday," he said while Annise made a wish and blew out the candle.

After slicing the cake, the steward gave a piece to everyone.

Annise looked around, puzzled. "Who told the cook today is my birthday?" No one admitted telling the cook, but she suspected it was her parents. *They love me, after all.*

Chapter 19

On the morning of the third day after their rescue, the refugees stood on the aft deck watching the Irish countryside pass. They slowly sailed up the Suir River in a gentle southerly wind.

Sailors stood on the ratlines of the yards, waiting for the captain's command. Once given, they quickly clawed the sails up and tied them to the yards. The momentum propelled the ship gently against the pilings, where the seamen secured the lines.

The dockworkers admired the skillful handling of the ship and applauded. Captain Young stepped off the vessel with a big smile and a friendly wave. He sought the foreman of the yard and inquired about getting his vessel hauled out.

"Yes," Patrick, the foreman, said. "We just launched a ship yesterday and are expecting none others at the moment. You caught us at the right time. A leak you say? Well now, you know we have to pull off all the copper sheeting to find it. I suppose you need a total caulk job with oakum and pitch. You all will be laid up for a while, but—" He rubbed his hands. "—we have some wonderful pubs in town."

"I also have some French refugees aboard. Is there a hotel in town?"

"Mrs. McGilley has a few rooms for rent. How many you need?"

"Two or three, I would say."

"That can be taken care of for sure. Now before we get started, I hate to ask you this, but I need to see you have money to pay me before we launch the ship."

Captain Young pulled a small leather bag out of his breast pocket and opened it. He reached in and pulled out some gold coins.

Patrick's face lit up, "We can get the cradle ready and haul the baby up this afternoon." He started shouting commands to his crew of workmen. "Now that you are in Ireland, let me wish you a hearty welcome, also let me recommend you go to the pub and order some Guinness ale."

"Any particular pub?"

"The Horse You Came In On is my favorite, but they are all good."

The five French refugees were delighted to feel solid earth beneath their feet again.

"I have never been so happy to put my shoes onto raw soil," said Azelma.

"Are we having an earthquake?" Annise said. "I feel the earth moving."

"You still have your sea legs," said her father. "You need to get used to being on land again."

They saw the captain standing nearby and went to him. Azelma spoke for the group. "Captain Young, we wish to thank you, for all you have done for us. As you know, the English Channel would have swallowed all of us. We would like to pay you for the food and lodging."

"It is the law of the sea, to help a mariner in distress. I was happy the Lord sent me to you when I was most needed. You owe me nothing. However, should you be in the pub when my men are there, I am sure, they would appreciate if you buy them a round or two."

"That we shall be happy to do," said Azelma before she interpreted for the others. "We shall be seeing you around town, I suppose."

"I'm sure our paths will cross. Goodbye for now."

"*Au revoir,*" the Frenchmen said with a wave and started toward the town of Passage East.

Sami caught up with them. "The captain sent me to help you find Mrs. McGilley's house."

After inquiring from a lady carrying her shopping basket, they were directed to the right house. Problem was, Mrs. McGilley spoke Gaelic and very little English. She went to a neighbor who could interpret for her. After a long time and many interpretations, the refugees rented two rooms for at least one night. One room was to be occupied by the three men and the other by Annise and her mother. Behind the house ran a brook.

"Is there a shop where we can buy some clothes?" Azelma asked the neighbor.

She directed them to a small general store not too far away. All five of them walked there, and the men quickly chose pants that tied below the knees, several white linen shirts, vests, sweaters, and several pairs of hand-knitted wool socks. They were unable to buy ready-made shoes, so decided to just keep using the ones they wore until they had a chance to go to the shoemaker.

The women had several garments to choose from, and were taking their time shopping. Meanwhile, the men hurried back to the rooming house, hoping to take a bath before the women returned. After much gesturing to Mrs. McGilley, she finally understood that the men wanted to take a bath. She took them outside and pointed to the creek.

Gabriel put his hand into the water. "Brrr," was all he said.

"But bathe we must," Peter exclaimed, starting to remove his clothes and slowly lowering his body into the water. "Once you are in, it really is not so bad."

"I shall ask Mrs. McGilley for soap," Eduard said,

starting toward the house. A short time later, he returned with soap and towels and joined the other two in the creek.

They washed their hair and bodies in a deep part of the brook without lingering. Once finished, they entered their room through a back door unseen by the landlady. With joy, they dressed in their new clothes and went outside. Peter watched in the direction of the general store, and, when he saw the women emerge, rushed toward them.

"Do you lovely lasses need help carrying your purchases?"

The women looked up with surprise. "Peter, you look so different. When I was not looking right at you, I did not realize it was you."

"Yes, we took an invigorating bath. I believe, with the dirt, also some years washed away."

"You must show me that bath. I would not mind losing a few years, especially the last few months."

"This is where we bathed," Peter said as they walked along the brook. "Right next to the house is a private spot."

"As soon as we get there," Azelma said. "I will discard these rags and bathe."

"I cannot wait to wash my hair," Annise added, "And put on my new garments."

Peter smiled. "You both will need courage, but I know you have it."

"What do you mean, my husband?"

"You shall see," he said, handing each one a linen towel and some soap. "I will be nearby and stand guard."

Peter had his back turned to the women. It was not long before he heard Annise gasp as she went into the water.

"Come in, Mama, the water feels good once you are used to it."

I wager the water is really cold. They think I will not go in, but they will get a surprise. Azelma jumped in, making a big splash.

Back in the room, they dressed. Both donned white linen blouses and white petticoats. Azelma put on a black wool vest laced in the front with a long green skirt attached. The front slit was open showing the white linen underskirt. Annise wore a black and green checkered full skirt with a separate black linen vest. Both women were able to buy comfortable brown leather shoes with low heels.

"My body is still tingling from that cold water," Azelma remarked.

"You still are pink and look young, Mama. What should I do with my hair?"

"Why don't you just braid it and let it hang? That is what I shall do with mine." Azelma turned around a few times and felt her skirt bell. "I feel young. Now I really appreciate how good it feels to be alive."

Hand in hand, they stepped outside where the men gave them admiring looks.

"You both look like beautiful Irish lasses," Peter said. "I am the luckiest man to have you ladies to take to dinner."

He extended his elbow and Azelma slipped her arm into his. Eduard did the same and Annise started walking with him. Gabriel walked a step behind, until Annise turned around and motioned for him to take her other arm. Annise felt like a queen with a handsome man on each arm. After a short walk they arrived at The Horse You Came In On. The proprietor greeted them as soon as they stepped in and escorted them to a long table. As soon as they were seated, a glass mug with dark brown liquid was placed in front of them.

"What is that?" Peter said.

"Guinness," the innkeeper said.

"*Nous voulons manger*," Peter said, motioning to his mouth with his hands.

The man gave them a confused look.

"We would like to eat," Azelma said.

The innkeeper's face lit up, and he rushed into the kitchen. Soon he returned with plates of boiled potatoes and fish and some cooked spinach. He watched with delight as the strangers dug into the food, especially the spinach.

While they ate, people filled the pub. Many were American seamen who enjoyed having other than ship's fare. The locals came with wives and children, most only drank the ale.

Soon men and women came carrying violins and small accordions. The locals squeezed together on the benches with the Frenchmen and started talking with them. Most of the locals were speaking Gaelic, the Frenchmen spoke French and English and no one understood the words. The feeling of love and respect was conveyed beyond the language barrier. Azelma was not used to being in close contact with anyone other than her family. Here she was, sitting next to people and enjoying it, even though some were not too familiar with soap and water.

The music played, and soon everyone began to sing. They locked arms and swayed in time with the music while sitting on the bench. By the second song, the French attempted to sing along with the encouragement of the locals. People got up to dance, and Annise and Eduard joined them. Eduard held her close as they swayed in time. Annise looked with apprehension toward her parents expecting disapproval. To her surprise, they both smiled. When the band played a fast song, the dancers broke apart and jumped into fancy steps, pounding their feet onto the wooden floor, trying to make as much noise as possible.

Eduard and Gabriel remained on the dance floor, imitating the men dancing, while Annise sat next to her mother.

"*Mere,* it is good seeing you and *Pere* enjoying yourselves."

"I cannot recall more fun. This is even better than a ball at Versailles. Here we are, spending the evening dancing and drinking and laughing with common people. It does make one think, maybe being an aristocrat is not all that great." Azelma jumped out of her seat. "I need to try this dance too," she shouted and joined the men and few women on the dance floor.

Peter got up and joined them, trying to learn Irish step dancing.

Eduard and Annise had stepped outside to look at the sky with the waning moon.

"Do you think we will be missed?" she said, melting into his embrace.

"Not for the time it takes to kiss you." He placed his lips on her eager mouth and felt her body respond with her rolling hips. "Oh, sweetheart, I love you so much. I would like to taste every inch of your body."

"And I wish to do the same to you." She took a step back. "Was not that bath today wonderful? You would never believe my mother actually jumped into the cold water."

"She did? And she did not scream with the cold?"

"No, she did not. I have never seen my mother as alive as today."

"There you are," Peter said. "You should see how well Gabriel is dancing. Come inside, before the musicians pack up and go home."

"*Oui, Pere.*" She whispered to Eduard, "Another time, and we shall get together."

It was almost midnight when the music stopped and the tavern emptied. The five Frenchmen walked back to the guest house, locking arms five across.

"This has been an eye-opening experience," said Azelma. "It puts life into a whole new perspective."

"What do you mean?" said Peter.

"I need to get sleep now. We need to talk tomorrow."

Outside the bedroom doors, Peter gave his wife a kiss and said in English, "Goodnight dear."

"Goodnight, sleep tight. I can hardly wait for the sun to rise again. I want to experience Ireland to the fullest."

Chapter 20

The next morning, everyone gathered at the table for breakfast, prepared by Mrs. McGilley. There were hard-boiled eggs, rolls, blood sausage, with coffee and tea. The men woke in a jovial mood and kept up a lively conversation about the pleasures of an Irish pub. Anise and Azelma ate without speaking.

After a while, Peter asked his wife, "You certainly are quiet, my dear. Are you feeling well?"

"Yes, I am feeling well," Azelma said. "Matter of fact, I am better than well. Peter, you will think me insane, but with everything that has happened to us in the past few months, I now have a totally different outlook on life."

"I am sure we all have. What is it you are thinking?"

"Peter, I am tired of traveling. Now that we are here, I see no reason not to just stay in Ireland."

"Of course, we can stay here for a week or two and rest up before we continue to England."

"I do not wish to go to England," Azelma said, rubbing her chin. "I really have no desire to see the marquis and the haughty marquise and force Annise to marry their milk-livered son...ah...whose name escapes me at the moment."

"Lukas," Peter added. "But we can stay with them in the castle, until we find a place of our own."

"Have you not heard anything I said?" Azelma said, standing up and leaning over the table. "I do not want to go to England. I have never felt so happy and welcome in a place as I did last night, surrounded by common and mostly unwashed people. Everyone made us feel welcome and wanted and loved."

"Are you saying you want to live in Ireland like a commoner?" Peter said with furrowed brow.

"How many ways do you want me to say it? Yes, Peter, I want to stay here, and I want you to give your blessings to Annise and Eduard."

Annise and Eduard sat next to each other, holding hands, and looked into each other's eyes with shining faces. Azelma sat down, put her arms around her daughter's shoulders, and started to speak, but no words escaped her lips. All she could do was give the girl a hug and nod, while tears streamed down her cheeks. Annise let go of Eduard's hand and flung her arms around her mother. With a choking voice, she whispered, "*Merci, Mama, merci.*"

The men sat in silence and just looked at the two women. Another young lady with a coffee pot in her hand walked into the room.

"Good morning," said the pretty girl dressed very much like Annise. "Would anyone care for more coffee?"

"Yes, I would," said Azelma. "Anyone else?" The three men held out their mugs for the girl to fill. "What is your name?" Azelma asked.

"I am Colleen, Mrs. McGilley's daughter."

Gabriel gave her an especially friendly look, wishing he could speak with her.

"Colleen," said Azelma, "Tell us something about the area. Are there any big cities nearby?"

"Yes, there is Waterford only about eight miles away. It is a nice city by the river. My husband is a glassblower at the crystal factory there."

When her words were translated, Gabriel gave a brief look of disappointment.

"Is there a reason we cannot make an outing to Waterford today?" Azelma suggested with sparkling eyes and flushed face.

Peter nodded.

"How is the best way to get to Waterford?" Azelma asked the girl.

"You can hire a horse and carriage at the livery stable."

"Is it far from here?"

"Nothing is far in this town," said Colleen. "But I suggest you go quickly to get one. With all the Americans in town, they will suck up all the resources. Of course, we are glad to have them. They bring money we desperately need."

"We better get ourselves a carriage right away, and make our way into the city," Azelma said, getting up and heading toward the bedroom.

Annise followed, and both women retrieved their cloaks. Annise still had the burden to wear the one heavy with coins and jewelry. "I hope I will not need to wear this cloak much longer."

"I thank you for being so diligent and keeping our fortune safe. I have removed a number of coins, and your father carries those."

"Yes, I did notice the cloak to be somewhat lighter."

Outside, the men were waiting. At the stable, they rented not only a carriage and two horses but also a driver. With high spirits, everyone climbed into the carriage and delighted in the ride along the river. They watched with fascination as the ships were loaded with whole sides of beef and mutton.

"Where are the ships going?" Azelma asked the driver in English.

"Some to the continent and others to

Newfoundland," the driver said proudly. "We have a lively trade with Canada."

"What do they bring back from overseas?" was Peter's first question.

"As far as I know, lumber and animal fur. See that gray tower over there? That's Reginald's Tower. They say it was built by the Vikings. Still being used today."

"What is it used for?" Gabriel asked before Peter could get a word out.

"It used to be a castle, a fortress and, in the fifteenth century, it was a mint. I think, now they use it to store ammunition."

"We are so fortunate to have you as our driver," said Azelma. "May we invite you for lunch in a pub?"

"You certainly may," he said with a two-fingered salute. "There is a good place overlooking the river on the next block."

On the way, they passed a thatch-roofed cottage. It was a one-and-a-half story white house with windows of the upper story looking like two eyes with its curved dormer. A sign in the front announced *to let*.

"Peter," Azelma said grabbing his arm with a vengeance, "Look."

"What is wrong?"

"Nothing is wrong. Look at that house. It is calling to me."

"That is only a little cottage."

"It is for rent. Just think. We could live there." She

raised her voice into a higher pitch. "Peter, it is perfect. We could rent that house and stay here. Please say you want it. Look, there is even an apple tree in full bloom right next to the cottage. I can see us now, eating and cooking with ripe apples."

"You have no idea what the inside looks like. It might be full of spiders and vermin."

"The outside looks neat and clean, I wager the inside is the same. Maybe someone at the pub knows how we can get in touch with the owner and see it."

"If that is what you really want," Peter said, with a puzzled but loving expression, "we shall see about it."

Annise and Eduard looked at each other with bright eyes. "I hope you can be my wife soon," he whispered.

"It looks like it might happen." She put her lips close to his, and he responded with a kiss.

"If we stay here," Azelma said, "The marquis will never have to know where we are. As far as they know, we just disappeared off the face of the earth."

"I would like to let Aunt Melina know we are alive," Annise said. "But we can request she keep it a secret. If de Castellane's eventually find out where I am, I will long be married with a number of babies."

Peter laughed. "I can just see myself a grandfather with five little ones on my lap."

The six people entered the mostly empty pub. Azelma and Peter immediately went to the man behind the bar. "Do you know who owns the cottage in the next block that is to let?"

"Eh?" said the man raising a cane with an attached ear trumpet and put the listening piece to his ear. "What did you say?"

"*DO YOU KNOW WHO OWNS THE HOUSE FOR LET IN THE NEXT BLOCK?*"

"No need to shout, little lady. I know who owns it."

"*THEN TELL*—pardon, then tell me, how I can find that person."

"You are looking at him. It is my house."

"We are interested in renting it," she said, placing her hand on Peter's shoulder.

"Would you like to see it?"

"Yes, very much so."

He took a key off a hook behind the bar, called to an unseen person in the kitchen to keep an eye on the pub. He walked out the door followed by the five Frenchmen like a mother duck leading her brood.

Azelma was closest to the man named O'Leary and walked abreast with him. "What can you tell us about the house?"

The middle-aged man held the ear trumpet to his ear. "Eh? Walk on the other side of me."

"What can you tell us about the house?"

"I lived in it with my family. Sad to say my wife died last year and the five kids are grown and married, and many moved away. That house is too big for me alone. I am happy with just a room above my pub.

O'Leary unlatched the wooden gate in a stone wall surrounding the garden. "That tree gives good apples, and more trees are in the back. He opened the wooden door of the cottage and showed them into the small foyer. On the left stood a door ajar leading into the parlor containing plain but sturdy furniture. He opened the door to the right, leading into the kitchen. It contained a wood-fired cooking stove, a stone sink with a brass hand pump, and a large cupboard displaying dishes and glassware. A long wooden table stood in the middle surrounded by benches and chairs.

"How much is the rent?" asked Peter.

"Five pounds a year," Azelma announced to everyone. "We can afford that, do you not agree, my husband? It would be perfect for us."

"We have not even seen the upstairs," Peter said, scratching his head, following his wife up the steps. Upstairs were three bedrooms fully furnished. "Go ahead, tell the man we shall lease the place, if that will make you happy."

"Thank you, Peter," Azelma said giving him a hug and kiss. She ran downstairs where the landlord was waiting. "We shall rent it."

"The rent is a year in advance," he said, scrutinizing their dress and wondering. "Do you have that much money?"

Peter handed the man a gold coin.

"I hope this is acceptable currency?" Azelma said.

"That is more than enough," said O'Leary. "I am an honest man, and I will give you some Irish money for change. Welcome to the city of Waterford. Come to my pub, and I hope you stay for lunch."

"To eat, is what brought us into the neighborhood in the first place," said the countess.

The five Frenchmen and the Irish driver sat around a table in the pub over the mid-day meal. The conversation was only in French, the driver concentrated on his plate of potatoes and corned beef with gravy. Annise sat close to Eduard and gave him sly and loving glances.

"I wonder," she whispered, "if that third bedroom was meant for you?"

Azelma looked at her daughter and announced, "Eduard, it would not be proper if you sleep in our house. We need to find you a room in town to rent."

At that moment, O'Leary brought more ale to the table.

"Mr. O"Leary—"

"Wait." He held the cane with the ear trumpet to his head. "What do you need?"

"Do you know of any rooms to let for this young man here?"

"I have a few empty rooms upstairs. Do you wish to see them?"

"I will take a look. Tell me, Mr. O'Leary, is there a newspaper in this city?"

"We certainly have one. There is the *Waterford Chronicle*. Come, follow me."

Chapter 21

W hen do you think we should move into the house?" Peter asked his wife.

"Why not this afternoon? The little we have at the room, the boys can bring to us tomorrow." Azelma took a deep breath. "You, Peter, sleep in one bedroom, I sleep in the other, and Annise can have the third. That is how we have always done it."

"Maybe we should change that," Peter said, lowering his voice. "I liked sleeping close to you as we did in the tower and on the boat."

Azelma giggled, as Eduard came back downstairs, with the landlord. "We can discuss that another time."

"There are some nice rooms upstairs," Eduard said, "And one of them would suit me well. My problem is, I need to borrow some money to pay the rent."

"I will give you the money," Peter said, reaching into his leather purse.

"No, I only want to borrow it. Mr. O'Leary believes I can get a job at the newspaper," Eduard said, indicating the landlord standing next to him.

Mr. O'Leary put the trumpet to his ear. "What did you say?"

"I told Mr. Brisson that I believe I can get a job at the *Chronicle*."

"Pickle you want, Yes, I do have some. They go good with the Guinness." He went into the kitchen to get the commodity.

"How much do you need for the rent?"

"If you lend me a shilling, it would suffice for a while."

Peter handed the young man a silver coin.

"Thank you. Now I have a more important question." Eduard sat back down next to Annise and took her hand. "Have you and your dear wife decided to give us your blessings?"

Peter looked at the young man. "Do you really love our daughter?"

"Sir, I was willing to risk my life for her. I fell in love the first moment I saw her at Chateau de Partie. My love for her deepened over the weeks. Time away from her was torture, and time close with her is almost heaven.

Even while we were bailing the boat together, I wanted to be nowhere else in the world, except next to her."

"And you did not defile her," Azelma said. "In spite of you being in close contact at times?

"No, I would be lying if I told you the thought was not there, but we took no action."

"I am happy to hear that," Peter said.

Eduard gave Annise's hand a squeeze. "Over the last few weeks, my love for her has grown. She is so brave, like her parents, and I feel she is my soulmate. My love for her will never die, only increase with time."

"Young man," Peter said, touching his wife's hand on the table. "If it was not for you, Azelma and I would now be in some mass grave with our head between our legs. We give our blessings for you two to get married."

Annise jumped up and hugged and kissed first her father then her mother. "*Merci, merci*, I love you both." Next she hugged Gabriel who had been sitting at the table silently, watching the drama unfold. "Thank you again, Gabriel, we could not have done it without your help."

Tears of joy came to Annise's eyes. Azelma rose and gave Eduard a hug, "Welcome to the family," she said, starting to cry.

The driver sat watching, not understanding a word, wondering what all the crying and hugging was about. Mr. O'Leary came to the table with a small bowl of pickles.

"We are going to have a wedding," Azelma said.

"These two young people are getting married."

"A wedding? You are going to have a wedding soon? That is wonderful," Mr. O'Leary said, clapping his hands. "I tell you what we can do. You can have the reception right here in my pub. We can decorate the place, and make it a wonderful feast. I love a wedding. It will be so much fun." He waved his cane with the ear trumpet into the air and shouted, "*WE ARE GOING TO HAVE A WEDDING.*"

Annise and Eduard looked at each other, and their faces lit up with radiant smiles. "We have to go about the business right away," she said. "We do not want to disappoint the landlord."

Peter rose and sat next to Eduard on the bench. "I too want to welcome you into the family. There is a dowry for Annise you will get once you are married. It is enough to get you two started."

"Sir, I expect to work and support Annise. It likely will not be to the standard she had in France, but I will do everything in my power to make her life easy and happy."

"*Oui*, Papa, all I want is to live with Eduard. We do not need a palace to be happy. Look at Mama. She lived in a palace all her life, and now she only wants to live in a cottage."

"You are right, my daughter," Azelma said. "The humblest home can be a palace when there is true love."

Gabriel cleared his throat, and everyone looked at

him. "I suppose my returning to France is now out of the question."

"Yes," Peter said, "I am sorry to disrupt your life. What do you plan on doing?"

"It was not much of a life with that cursed occupation. Now I too have the opportunity to start fresh."

"This looks like an active city," Azelma observed. "You can get a job here doing something."

"I plan to speak with Captain Young, with the help of Sami or Remi of course, and ask if I can get a job on the ship. When we get to America, I can decide what to do."

"My Friend," Eduard said, "I hope you will be here for our wedding."

"If it is before the ship sails, I will be there. Provided they let me sail with them, of course."

Eduard took a deep swallow and emptied his mug. "When you get to America, you will have to write to us and tell us all about it."

Peter held his mug in the air and, when O'Leary glanced his way, he called, "Another round, please."

"Your English is improving," Azelma commented.

O'Leary brought six mugs to the table and set one in front of each person.

"Thank you," Eduard said. "Starting now, I will speak as much English as I can."

"Yes, we need the practice," Annise said, standing

up. She quickly sat back down and put her head on her arms. "*Je me sens ivre*," she whispered.

"She feels tipsy," Eduard said. "We better take her to the cottage right away and let her rest."

"Good thought," said her mother. "That will ensure we move in today."

Everyone helped Annise first into the carriage for the short ride to the cottage. There she half walked, was half carried by both Eduard and her father to a bedroom where she could rest on a wide bed. Eduard bent over her and kissed her on the lips,

"Now rest, my love, I shall be back tomorrow. Just think, today is our engagement day. May second, a date to remember."

Annise did not respond. She was sleeping.

Gabriel and Eduard took off in the carriage toward Passage East.

Once alone, Peter took Azelma into his arms. "Privacy at last. Do you realize where we were the last time we did it?"

"That I will never forget. It seems forever since we have been in the tower. We have traveled a long way and have had a half a lifetime of experiences behind us."

"And now we can make another lifetime of experiences." He kissed her with passion. She returned the kiss and responded by pressing her hips close to his body.

Chapter 22

The next day, a Saturday, Eduard knocked on the door of the cottage in Waterford. Annise opened the door, looking fresh and bright, dressed in her Irish garb. She had combed her hair back and tied it at the back of her head with a green ribbon. Large waves of blonde tresses trailed down her back and curled on the end. When she saw Eduard, her eyes brightened, but when she looked past him, she squealed with delight. "What a beautiful horse."

She ran toward the gray animal and stroked her black mane. The horse snorted in a friendly manner.

After giving Annise a lengthy hug, he said, "Are you ready to go with me to church, and find a priest?"

"I have been ready for a long time now. Come in.

My parents are having a late breakfast. They plan to go to church too." They both went into the kitchen and approached the count and countess.

"*Bonjour,* no, good morning," Azelma said. "Would you like some bread and blood sausage?"

"No thank you. I am eager to find a priest this morning. I have come with my steed to whisk my lady-love into married bliss. I could see the steeple of a Catholic church on my way here. It is not far."

"Are you sure it is Catholic?" asked Peter.

"I believe so. It has a cross on top."

"You two go ahead. Her mother and I will walk over after we finish eating." Peter looked at his wife. "Do you feel like walking?"

"It is a lovely day to be alive and able to go walking with my handsome husband."

Peter chuckled and saw the young people to the door. "I think he will make her a good husband," he said, taking his place at the table.

Azelma smiled and reached for his hand. "As good as mine."

༺༻

The pommel of the saddle was low, and Annise could sit in comfort with both legs down on one side of the horse. Edward sat in the saddle and held her as the Connemara pony slowly walked on the streets toward the church. Arriving at the large white building with the high steeple, they dismounted, hitched the horse to a post, and went in. They were surprised at the plainness of the interior and wondered if it was a Catholic Church. The only other person visible was an old lady, sitting in a pew near the front and praying.

The old lady started for the door in the back of the church when Eduard asked her in English, "Where might we find a priest?"

The old lady shrugged her shoulders and spread her arms, saying something they did not understand.

"There is a priest now," Annise said, pointing toward the altar.

They rushed toward him, and Eduard cleared his throat. "Excuse me, Father, we want to get married. Can you do that?"

"Are you a member of the Church of Ireland?" asked the clergyman.

"No, Father," said Eduard. "We arrived from France yesterday. This is Annise de Brisson and I am Eduard Saulnier. Her parents have rented a cottage here in Waterford."

"Since you come from France, I assume you are of the Roman Catholic faith. There is a brand new Roman Catholic cathedral on Barronstrand Street. It is called the Cathedral of the Most Holy Trinity. You need to inquire there."

"Could you point the way?"

"Yes, when you get outside, make a right until you get to the end of the street, then turn left and left again on Barronstrand Street. You will see it then."

As the two young people stepped out of the cathedral, the count and countess approached them. "Did you find a priest?" asked Azelma.

"This is a Protestant church. There is a new Catholic cathedral nearby. Shall we walk over together?"

"And who will ride this fine steed?" Peter asked no one in particular. "If all of you are going to walk, I shall make use of the horse. I shall meet you at the church." He mounted the horse and rode off.

"I believe Peter missed his horse more than anything while we were in prison," Azelma said with a half-hearted shrug. "Chances are, he will get lost and miss the meeting with the priest."

They walked along Barronstrand Street, looking for a building that looked like a cathedral.

"Look at that beautiful building across the street," Annise said. "That must be the opera house."

Eduard and Annise kept walking, hand in hand, giving each other loving glances.

After a while, he remarked, "According to what the minister at the church said, we should have seen the cathedral a while ago. We better ask that lady coming this way if she can help us. Excuse me, could you tell us, where the Cathedral of the Most Holy Trinity is?"

"Yes, she said, pointing to where they had come from, "It is back about four blocks."

"That was a church?" Eduard said. "We thought it was an opera house."

"Oh no." The middle-aged lady laughed. "There is no opera house. We only have a theater."

"Thank you for your help," said Azelma and they hurried toward the church.

They arrived at the new square building with pillars in front reminiscent of a Greek temple. On closer inspection, they realized the five statues on the roof represented apostles. The familiar gray horse was tied to the hitching post in front.

"I see Peter found the place before we did," said Azelma as they started up the steps.

Once they entered the building, they knew they were in a Catholic Church. Near the altar in the front of the church sat Peter, talking with a priest. They went forward to join them.

Peter looked up with a bright smile. "You will never guess who is here. It is Father Pierre. You remember him from our parish in Paris."

"Father Pierre," said Azelma, making a curtsy in front of him. "It is wonderful seeing you. We had no idea you were in Ireland."

"Yes, my child, it is wonderful seeing you too, Countess de Brisson. I had to make a quick exit because I refused to accept the new Religion of Reason. It was either exile or the guillotine. As you can see, I chose the former. I am one of the assistant priests in this beautiful new cathedral. What brings you to Ireland?"

"On our way to the guillotine, this young man named Eduard Saulnier and two of his friends, rescued us," Peter said. "We traveled by boat down the Seine and attempted to cross the English Channel. The Lord and all that is holy smiled on us and sent an American ship to rescue us. That ship is now in dry-dock in Passage East, and yesterday we rented a cottage in Waterford."

"Yes," added Azelma, "Never in a thousand years would we have ever expected to live in Ireland. But on our first day here, we decided to settle down, at least for a while."

"And now you are here in this brand new cathedral to thank God for sparing your life," added the priest.

"Yes, and to arrange for these young people to get married," Peter added with pride.

The priest looked at Annise's glowing face with her bright hopeful eyes. He turned his gaze to the young man and saw the sincere love in his face. "When do you want to get married?"

"As soon as possible," answered Eduard.

"In Ireland, you cannot rush into marriage," said the gray-haired priest. *There is something I should remember about these people. I don't remember what it is. If God wills it, it will come to me.* "In Ireland, it takes at least three months."

"Three months?" Eduard said, stiffening his back. "Why so long?"

Annise slumped into herself and gave a soft moan. The brightness suddenly left her eyes.

"Legalities for one. You have to present yourself before a magistrate and apply for a license. Then the church requires banns, but that is only for a month. The bishop requires you to have pre-marriage counseling with a priest."

What does a celibate person know about marriage? Eduard wondered. "If that is what it takes to make Annise my wife, I will be glad to do all, that is required."

"How old are you two?"

"I am twenty-two and Annise—" he said, taking her hand, "—is eighteen."

"You are old enough. If you were any younger, you would need your parent's consent."

"And that she would have," Peter said.

"I will do anything it takes to make Annise my wife. Please, Father, tell us exactly what we must do to marry in three months."

"Are you Catholic?"

"Yes, Father," Eduard answered with a slight hesitation.

"When is the last time you were in confession?"

"I have not been since I left Paris." *That is the truth, but I am not saying how long ago was my last confession.*

"None of us had confession lately," Azelma added.

"That will be the first order of business. I am free right now to hear your confessions. After that, I can start the process of getting these young people married."

❧❧❧

A few days later, the priest received a letter from a friend in England. It made him remember what had escaped him, when he was talking with the Brissons. As soon as he had time, he wrote to his friend.

Chapter 23

Once the legalities of getting married were begun, there was not much else to do but plan the festivities for the wedding. The French refugees hired a local school teacher to give them English lessons. Azelma improved her writing skills and even learned some Gaelic. The locals accepted them as friends and neighbors, unaware they were nobility. Dinner invitations were readily exchanged, and the countess and Annise produced some fine meals for their new friends.

Captain Young hired Gabriel as an apprentice sailor. He spent his days learning the ropes along with English. Both Sami and Remi were his teachers.

Eduard inquired at the *Waterford Chronicle* for employment. He was hired to draw caricatures. It did not take long and his English was good enough for him to go out and gather information and write articles. As soon as he had enough earned money, he went to a jewelry store and bought a Claddagh ring for Annise.

One evening at the O'Leary pub, when the band was taking a rest, a man placed a chair in the middle of the dance floor. Eduard took Annise's hand, led her to the chair, and motioned for her to be seated.

All eyes of the patrons were watching as Eduard knelt in front of her and spoke in a clear voice, "Annise, my one and only love, in front of all these witnesses, I again ask you to be my wife. Please, make me the world's happiest man, and accept me."

She looked at him with hesitation. She bit her lower lip and made eye contact with her parents then panned her gaze over everyone in the room. All laughter stopped, and the people looked at her in silence. With hesitation, Eduard opened the ring box and showed her the golden ring. A minute went by. She jumped to her feet and shouted, "Yes, *oui, ja, si*, I will be honored to be your wife."

She pulled him up and hugged him, as if she never wanted to let go.

He slipped the ring on the finger of the left hand with the heart toward the fingernail. "Wearing it like that shows we are engaged. After the wedding, the ring is turned with the heart toward your own. *Merci,* my love, for accepting me."

All the people in the pub crowded around the young couple and gave them hugs and good wishes. Peter offered to buy everyone drinks, and that produced a big cheer with congratulations to the parents. They were saved from being crushed by the band playing a happy jig that made people rush onto the dance floor. In the wee hours of the morning, people went home, and Eduard almost crawled up the steps to his room.

When he removed his vest and pants, his manhood greeted him. "Six more weeks of tranquility and then you can enjoy yourself. I know you are eager, but you will just have to wait."

ecseo

As spring made way for summer, the wedding preparations were close to fruition. A dressmaker worked on Annise's wedding dress of fine light blue linen with a split skirt. Azelma made a strong suggestion that the underskirt and blouse should be nothing less than silk. They ordered the material from a fabric outlet in London. Twice a week the mail coach passed through Waterford. It was on one of those days Annise waited for the coach, hoping to receive the package with silk.

Before the coach came into sight, the sound of the horn alerted everyone, the coach was near and to get out of the way.

The local postmaster waited with a sack of mail,

ready to toss it to the armed guard sitting next to the driver. That day the coach slowed down and stopped near where Annise was standing.

Oh good, the coach is stopping. I hope it is because they have my fabric.

The coach door opened and a young man emerged. The first thing Annise noticed was the fancy silver buckles on highly polished black shoes. White silk stockings emphasized his slim legs. Gold tassels dangled below his knees tying the legs of black pants. He wore a red wool jacket with tails and gold decorations on the lapels and cuffs. White lace edged ruffles were just visible above the bare hands. When Annise glanced at his face, she gave a soft gasp.

"Annise, you are here to meet me," said a surprised voice in French. "How did you learn I was coming?"

"I—I did not k—know it," she stammered. "I was waiting for a package."

All she could do was stand with her arms hanging limp at her sides, and stare at the handsome, clean shaved face and his short, dark brown, curly hair.

He reached for her hand and kissed it. Next, he reached into the coach and retrieved his tri-cornered hat and large leather bag.

"Thank you," he shouted to the coachman, "Carry on."

The coachman shook the reins of the four geldings and shouted to them. The horses took off at a gallop.

Annise watched them go, still speechless.

"Have you nothing to say to your fiancé?" he said in French.

"Lukas de Castellane," she muttered, wringing her hands, "What brings you to Waterford?"

"I had been informed that you are here. That is why I have come. My family and I have been so worried about you. The last communication we received about you was from your Aunt Melina. She wrote about your parents' arrest and possible pending execution. Then all of you disappeared to who knows where. We did not know if you were dead or alive. The first we learned what happened to all of you was when we received a letter from Father Pierre."

"In that case, I am sure he wrote the reason we came to see him."

"Yes, he did mention you are about to marry a commoner," he said, frowning then clenching his jaw. "I want to stop you from making the biggest mistake of your life."

How dare he say that? Marrying him would be the biggest mistake. I feel like slapping him in the face, but that is something I would not dare to do in public.

The attire of the stranger raised the curiosity of the locals. They made a circle around the two and listened intensely. Since they were speaking French, no one understood them, but each person interpreted their facial expressions and drew his own conclusion.

"Is there not a better place we can go to talk?"

"I beg your pardon for being rude," she said, her face becoming pink. "Come, we shall go to my parent's house. It is only a short walk from here."

The people parted and let them pass. Some were even so brazen and followed to see if there was any more drama.

When they arrived at the Brisson cottage, Lukas assumed the two people wearing peasant clothes and working in the garden in front of the house were hired help. He hardly looked at them until Annise called to them.

"*Mere, Pere,* look who is here. Can you believe that?"

Countess Azelma adjusted her straw bonnet and called, "Marquis de Castellane! What in the world brings you here?" She extended her hand, and he kissed the air above it. "Welcome to our humble abode."

"*Enchante, Comtese Azelma.*"

Peter walked toward the young man, wiped his right hand on his pants, and extended it.

Lukas took it somewhat reluctantly. "Count Peter, it is good to see you. When we left France a year ago, we wondered if we ever will see our friends again."

"Come into the house," Azelma said. "It is nice and cool. You are dressed so warm, and not a drop of perspiration on you. How do you stay so cool? Now tell us, what brings you here?"

"Before we get into a long conversation, Azelma, let the young man refresh himself with something cold to drink." Peter put his hand on Lukas's shoulder then noticed it left a dirt print.

"Is this where you live?" Lukas asked with raised eyebrows.

"Yes," Peter said as they walked in the front door. "Isn't it nice? We do have an extra bedroom. You can stay here. No, on second thought, we really do not have an extra room, but I can sleep with my wife while you stay with us."

"Thank you for the offer, but it might be better if I stay at an inn."

"Yes, there is a very nice and comfortable inn here in town," Azelma said with a hopeful smile. "Would you care for some tea or coffee?"

"*Merci,* some tea would taste good right now," Lukas said, taking a chair at the end of the kitchen table. "It is good seeing all of you well. Of course, my parents sent their greetings and a letter, telling about our trip to England. That was quite an ordeal traveling by boat across the channel. What is even worse, it took weeks to find a suitable palace to rent for our residence."

Annise just sat there gazing at the young man, thinking, *He thinks he had a rough time crossing the channel. He does not even ask how we got here. Is he not the least bit curious how my parents escaped the guillotine?*

"Those English castles are so dreary, compared to our French chateaus. I simply cannot wait for the government at home to straighten out and restore the king."

"Yes," Peter said. "We saw the dauphin when we were in the tower. He is a delightful child and so well behaved. I played ball with him."

"And I had some lovely conversations with the queen," added Azelma. "The poor woman is not doing well at all. And that sweet, darling princess. None of them deserve to be where they are."

Lukas looked at the count and countess with new respect. "You actually were imprisoned with the royal family? I had no idea you rated that high."

Peter looked at his wife with raised eyebrows. She just rolled her eyes with a just-let-it-pass expression.

Annise just sat there and twisted her Claddagh ring with her right hand. *Lukas always had a very regal demeanor, but now I see him as an insufferable snob. Thank God, my parents are not that way. If he insists he wants to marry me, I will tell him I am pregnant.*

"The reason I made this long journey," continued the marquis, rising and pacing the floor, "Is to claim my promised bride."

Annise's mouth flew open, and her face paled. She gave her father a pleading look.

Peter coughed. "Yes, I remember your father and I made that agreement over ten years ago. Now there is so much changed, and I honestly believed the agreement to be no longer valid."

"Count de Brisson," the marquis said in his most regal voice. "It is only invalid if both parties agree. Just the fact that I am here does not indicate that. I want to take Annise back with me and get married in England."

"You mean," Azelma said, "In all of England there is no young lady that pleases you enough to marry her?"

"I fell in love with Annise when we were children," he said, walking toward Annise and taking her hand. "Seeing her now, even though she is dressed like a peasant, I love her even more. When I look at her, I see how she would look in proper attire and wearing jewels. Now I want to restore her to her station in life and elevate her nobility." He kissed her hand and looked into her blue eyes. "Say you will have me and make me the happiest man."

"L—Lukas," she stammered. "I—I love Eduard and want to be his wife. You cannot imagine how much he has done for us."

"Of course, he has done things for you. That is the duty of commoners, to be subservient to us nobility. That does not mean you need to marry him. Where is the man now?"

"He is working for the *Waterford Chronicle*," Annise said, pulling her hand away from his. "He wants to earn money to support us."

"Ha, does that mean you will cook and clean and

wash his dirty underwear?" Lukas said with a sneer. "Will I get to meet the man who has such a hold on you?"

"As a matter of fact," Peter said, "I see him approaching the house right now."

Everyone looked out of the window and saw Eduard opening the garden gate.

He was dressed in brown pants that tied below the knees and a white long-sleeved shirt. A brown vest contained pockets and gave the casual outfit a somewhat dressy look. Under his arm, he carried a big white board.

Peter opened the front door and greeted the young man. *"Dia dhuit."* He hoped speaking Gaelic would make the haughty Lukas feel left out.

Eduard looked at all in the room and responded, *"Dia is Muire dhaoibh."*

"Eduard," Peter said. "Let me introduce Marquis Lukas de Castellane, he was our neighbor in France. He came all the way from England to visit us. Lukas, meet our good friend, Eduard Saulnier."

Eduard extended his hand. "An honor to meet you."

Lukas just touched his fingers and shook them without saying anything.

"What do you have under your arm?" Azelma wanted to know.

Eduard showed them a picture of the Cathedral of the Most Holy Trinity. "It is a new project I am working on. You like it?"

"Wonderful," Annise said. "That is a watercolor. Did you do it?"

"The answer is no and yes," Eduard said. "It is an aquatint, and yes, I did do it."

"How did you do that?" Peter said, wanting to talk about anything except the purpose of Lukas's visit.

"I did the engraving on copper and, due to the use of acids and timing, one can achieve different colors. I also had a picture of Reginald's Tower, but on my way over here, a man stopped me and offered to buy it right then and there. I must confess, for the time it takes to make it, and what I got for the etching, I can make more money than working for the newspaper." Eduard reached into his vest pocket and pulled out a gold coin.

"You got that for the picture?" Annise said, wide-eyed.

"Yes, I feel absolutely wealthy. I will get busy and make more in my spare time. My boss agreed to let me use the printing press at the newspaper. Of course, I offered to pay him for the use. Now I feel like celebrating. I invite all of you to O'Leary's for supper." He looked at Lukas, "Including you too, young man."

"Thank you," Azelma said, looking at all in the room. "I do not know about all of you, but I am getting hungry. Since we have been working in the garden all day, I did not cook anything. But in a few days, we can eat our own harvest."

Azelma washed her hands at the sink, followed by

Peter and Annise. Lukas ran some water over his fingertips.

"We are ready to go," Peter announced.

"You don't dress for dinner?" said Lukas.

Peter and Azelma looked at each other and laughed. "Our stomachs do not care what is on the outside, as long as we fill it with good food, and good food is to be had at O'Leary's. You, young man, will get quite a bit of attention in your attire. Maybe *you* would like to dress for dinner."

"The only other thing I have with me is fancier. I expected you to live in a palace. Where can I rent a room for tonight?"

"You need lodging?" Eduard said in a sarcastic tone. "There is an empty room at O'Leary's. I am certain it is not up to your standards since all the butlers are on vacation, but it is clean and more than adequate."

Annise went to Eduard. "I love that picture. Can we borrow it and hang it up, in our parlor for a while?"

"Of course you can." They all followed Eduard into the living room where he hung it on an empty nail above the mantle. "It looks like it belongs here."

Peter sighed. *I hope he does not bring up the fact this is the church they are going to be married in.*

"Annise and I will be married in that church."

"That is something I want to discuss," Lukas said.

"I hate to discuss on an empty stomach," Eduard said. "I could smell the corned beef roasting on my way here. Come, let us hurry before all the good tables are taken."

He reached for Annise's hand, and everyone left the house.

Lukas picked up his large leather bag and followed. *I cannot believe I am walking behind them like a dog.*

Chapter 24

O'Leary's pub quickly filled, since corned beef night was very popular. Not only did the cook boil the meat, but then glazed it with honey and spices and roasted it in the oven. It was served with potatoes, cabbage, sourdough bread, and butter. Most people washed the fare down with Guinness. It was not far into the evening when the music started, encouraging people to sing and dance.

At first, the locals did not know how to deal with the marquis in his fancy clothes and gave him space. After a while, some of the local girls cozied up to him and urged him to dance. They laughed at his attempts of the Irish jigs. With the help of several mugs of Guinness, Lukas took the laughter like a good sport and started enjoying himself. When he offered to buy a round for all in the house, he suddenly became everyone's closest friend. Thus the evening passed, without a discussion of why he was in Ireland. In the early hours of the morning, Eduard and Lukas climbed the stairs and went into their own rooms. Both were too exhausted to engage in a conversation.

The next morning, Lukas ate breakfast in the pub. The only other person there was Mr. O'Leary serving him two eggs with blood sausage and bread.

"How you like our sausage?" O'Leary asked, holding the ear trumpet next to his face.

"I have eaten better," said Lukas, looking at the dark red slice on his plate.

"You are right, we are having great weather. Now, how do you like the sausage?"

"It is good," Lukas said with a smile. "Hunger is the best cook."

"That is right, and I am so fortunate he works for me."

ⴵⴽⴵ

At the Brisson cottage, Azelma answered Lukas's knock on the door.

"I am sorry, but this is a bad time for a visit. Peter is under the weather and Annise is indisposed. I am sure both of them will feel better by this afternoon. Please come back then."

"Could you direct me to the cathedral? I would like to see Father Pierre."

"Of course," she said, walking him toward the street. "See that steeple there? That is not it. When you pass it, go to the end of the street and make a left to Barronstrand Street and make another left. The cathedral looks more like a theater than a church."

"Thank you, I shall return later. Hopefully, everyone will have recovered."

"I believe they will feel better."

Lukas leisurely wandered the streets of Waterford until he reached the cathedral. He was impressed by the elegant interior. *I thought of the Irish as backward people, but they do know how to build a decent church.* He walked up to the marble altar and saw Father Pierre, arranging the host for the next mass.

"Father Pierre, is it really you?"

The old man turned around, and his face broke into a big smile. "Lukas de Castellane, my son, how wonderful to see you."

Lukas rushed to the man, took his hand, and knelt down.

"Rise, my son, a hug will suffice. It does my heart good to see you. How are your dear parents and brothers and one sister, I believe?"

"They are well, Father, and sent you their warmest greetings. You are looking healthful. Ireland must agree with you."

"Thank you, my son, I left France just in time." said the priest, looking sad. "The Regime wanted me to abandon all Catholic beliefs and take on the Worship of Reason. Can you imagine? They want everyone to regress to pagan worship. I had a choice to either accept or off with the head. I told them, I was ready to convert and fled for England."

"Then what brings you to Ireland?"

"It is hard to make a living as a Catholic priest when all the churches are the Church of England. That is what brings me here. Observe," he said, with a sweep of his arm, "This cathedral is brand new, only completed this year."

"Beautiful," Lukas said, looking at the black marble Corinthian columns accented with gold leaf.

"Yes," said the priest. "It really makes me unhappy to think that all the beautiful churches in France are now Temples of Reason. All crosses and sacred pictures have been removed, not only from the churches, but also some cemeteries. They even started a new calendar making this year two."

"France is riddled with insanity," Lukas said, looking dejected. "We have no idea what state our beautiful palace is in. Do you think the king will ever be restored?"

"I have absolutely no insight of what will happen," said the priest, folding his hands and bowing his head. "All we can do is hope and pray this Reign of Terror will end soon, and France will again become the great nation, it once was. Now, young man, I am sure you did not come to see me to discuss politics. What is on your mind?"

"You might recall that Annise and I were promised to each other in marriage. I understand she now is betrothed to another man."

"And a fine young man he is," added the priest.

"But don't I have priority? She was engaged to me first."

"How long ago was that arrangement made?"

"A little over ten years now. I remember we were both eight years old at the time. The count and countess had a birthday party for her, and my family was among the guests. While we children were playing games on the lawn, our parents sat in a pergola drinking wine and talking. Soon Annise and I were called to come to them. My father informed us that now we were promised to each other in marriage."

"How did you feel when they told you that?"

"I was delighted. I felt so grown up to have a fiancée. We both were allowed to drink some wine to seal the agreement. I remember, we locked arms, drank a sip, and I kissed her on the lips, right there in front of everybody. Both of our parents clapped their hands and cheered."

"And do you think that engagement made for two young children is still valid across the English Channel and spanning many years?"

"Yes, why would it not be?" Lukas asked with a raised pitch to his voice and wide eyes.

"Because you are now in a different country and under different circumstances," said the priest, taking a quick breath. "How do you feel about her now? Do you still want to marry her?"

"She is beautiful."

"Is that all you can say about her? Just beautiful. Would you run into a burning building to save her life?"

"If it was safe to do so, and she was just lying there unconscious."

"Suppose there is a good chance that you would not get out alive when you ran in to save her?"

"In that case, I would stand outside and pray for her."

"That is not love you feel for her. Let me tell you— Eduard Saulnier risked his life to save the count and countess from the guillotine. Not only that, but they attempted to cross the English Channel in a small boat that sank. Had it not been for an American ship coming by to save them, all would now be on the bottom of the channel."

"I had no idea."

"You did not ask the count and countess how they got here?"

"We hardly had a chance to talk. We went to a pub, and surely you know how noisy that can be."

"I know. You are a handsome young man, who can choose from among many beautiful women to marry. Besides, you have a title and all the privileges to go with it. Be reasonable and let Annise and Eduard get married. Those two people share a love that only comes along infrequently. God has surely blessed them with it."

"But we were formally engaged in front of our parents and other witnesses. Does that not mean something?"

"What we can do is un-engage you," said Father Pierre. "We should be able to redress the situation after mass tomorrow."

"Un-engage?" Lukas said tilting his head to the right. "I have never heard of such a ceremony."

Neither have I, but if that is what he wants, that we shall do. At least that is a man whose word is still his honor. I will have to think of something. "Tomorrow, all of you come to the ten o'clock mass, and we shall have the ceremony immediately following service. I trust you will inform the Brissons."

"Yes, Father, I expect to see them this afternoon."

"Now, my son, when is the last time you had confession?"

"I am due for one."

"We can take care of that right now."

Chapter 25

Azelma sat in the parlor doing some embroidery when she saw Lukas approaching the house. *Oh, oh, I'm sure he is here to speak about the engagement.* No sooner had the thought come into her mind, than there was a knock on the door. Azelma answered it.

"Lukas," she said with a big smile, "How nice to see you again. Please come in."

"Are Count de Brisson and Annise feeling better?"

"Yes, they are. Both of them are out in the garden, picking some vegetables. We can go into the garden and join them."

"That is good. I have hardly spoken with them since I arrived."

They both stepped out of the back door and Azelma

called in a forced cheerful voice, "Look who is here."

Peter straightened up and smiled. He walked toward the young man, wiped his hands on his apron, and extended his right hand. "Good to see you, marquis."

"I am happy to see you feeling well again, Count de Brisson, and Annise looks sprightly."

"Yes, thank God. Come we shall sit in the shade and talk. Azelma, do we have anything cold to drink?"

"Yes, I shall get some cold tea. Annise, come and help me."

Annise gave Lukas a fleeting smile as she passed him on the way into the house.

Once seated under a canopy, Peter asked, "Now tell me, young man, what brings you all the way to Ireland?"

"Father Pierre wrote to my father that all of you are here. He was so happy to see you made it safely out of France and mentioned Annise is to be married."

"Yes, that is so."

"I believe we are still engaged."

"I was aware of that. But since we are no longer in France, I also believe that agreement is no longer valid."

"I intended to come and claim her as my bride." Lukas said, studying his hands. "But I had a long talk with Father Pierre."

Peter raised his eyebrows. "Oh, what did he say?"

"He explained to me what love between a man and woman means. He asked if I would risk my life for her. It made me think."

"And would you risk your life by running into a burning building?"

"That is exactly what he asked me too. My father always said that it is not necessary to love when getting married. The important thing is that she is a woman to have at the side that you are not ashamed to introduce as your wife. As long as she is up to our social standing, that is all that matters. If intimacy is good, that is a bonus. If it is not good, there are servants and concubines."

"That is where I disagree one hundred percent. My wife and I truly loved each other when we got married, and we have always been faithful to each other. She could have escaped when the mob raided our chateau, but she stayed at my side. I love that woman more than life itself."

"I envy you, and I envy Mr. Saulnier. I have never learned about love like that at home. What can you tell me about Eduard?"

"That young man risked his life and that of two of his friends to save us from the guillotine. If it was not for their bold actions, we would definitely be lying in a mass grave now. We are honored he loves our Annise, and, fortunately, she returns his love. We could not be more pleased than to see them get married."

"I had no idea you were condemned to die," Lukas said in an apologetic voice. "My father and mother left France because they could see the political climate deteriorating. When this disorder clears up, which my father is sure it will, they want to return to France and reclaim their chateau and land."

"If God wills it, we too might be able reclaim our land and chateau, but, meanwhile, we make our home here. Being in prison has taught us to be grateful for every small thing we have. We have everything that is important right here."

"What do you consider the most important possession?"

"We have each other as a family, we have full bellies and comfortable beds, and, as a bonus, we have the love and respect of our neighbors. Neither do we live in fear of someone coming to vandalize our home and kill us."

"Count de Brisson, I am learning so much from you. It made my trip worthwhile."

"Please, just call us Peter and Azelma. Our neighbors do not know we are nobility, and we want it to stay that way."

"I will respect your wishes."

Annise and her mother came into the garden, each carrying two glasses of cold tea with wedges of lemon.

"I am sure you men are thirsty," Azelma said. "Have you solved the world's problems yet?"

"Not all in the world," Peter said with a chuckle, "But maybe our personal ones."

"Oh?" Azelma said, raising one eyebrow. "What is it?"

"Lukas, is there something you want to tell Annise?"

"Annise," Lukas said rising and taking her right hand and kissing the back of it. "What I have to say to you, I will say in front of your parents. Annise, I wish you and Monsieur Saulnier much happiness in your married life. Tomorrow, after mass, Father Pierre wants to perform an un-engagement ceremony."

"That is it?" she said with a trembling voice and a slow smile. "Thank you."

"You look surprised," Lukas said. "Did you expect me to challenge Mr. Saulnier to a duel?"

"I—I did not know what to expect," she stammered, looking heavenward and letting out a deep breath. A big smile replaced her worried frown.

Lukas smiled and kissed her hand again. "As you can see, I am a reasonable man."

I am glad the dueling pistols can stay in the bottom of my bag. Now how will I explain this to my father? I know, I will just tell him that Annise and her parents have become commoners and are no longer aristocratic, and I did not want her anymore. As for myself, I cannot wait to get back to a palace, even an English palace.

"Lukas," Azelma said, "You will do us the honor and sup with us this evening. Annise and I will be cooking a stew."

"You cook yourself?" he said, surprised.

"Of course," Annise said, stepping back. "We manage to put a decent meal on the table. At home in France, I kept company with the cook and watched her.

She told me the importance of using the right spices."

"Eduard will be joining us," Azelma said. "Now you probably think we spend every evening at the pub. That is not so. We also enjoy quiet evenings at home playing cards or board games. While Annise and I are cooking, you and Peter can play a board game. Annise, why don't you get the mancala set?"

The two men started playing while the women went in to cook.

Azelma gave a sigh of relief. "I was afraid his visit might become nasty."

"If it would have come to that, I would have told him I am pregnant," Annise said. Azelma gave her daughter a startled look. Annise shrugged. "Of course I'm not, but Lukas has no way of knowing I'm still a virgin."

While the women cooked, Eduard knocked and entered the house. He greeted both ladies. Annise puckered her lips and motioned for him to kiss her. He looked at her mother who nodded and smiled.

After the kiss, Annise asked, "How was your day?"

"It went very well. I had finished my work for the paper early and stayed and worked on a new lithograph. My boss even has some friends who are interested in buying some. As it turns out, I have found a new way to make a living, and it might be a good living at that."

"That is wonderful," said Azelma. "We can eat soon, and the marquis will join us for supper."

Eduard looked out the back window and saw the two

aristocrats bent over a game board. "I can imagine what he came here for. Has that situation been resolved?"

"Yes, he spoke with Father Pierre, and this whole engagement situation has been worked out. Tomorrow after ten o'clock mass, the Father wants to perform an un-engagement ceremony."

"An un-engagement ceremony? I never heard of such a thing."

"Neither have I," Azelma continued with a chuckle. "I think the good father might have made that up. At least it is better than fighting a duel. Will you join us for mass tomorrow?"

"Yes, I plan to be there," Eduard said. "Your cooking smells wonderful."

"It is beef stew, and it's done," Azelma said testing with a fork. "Annise dear, please set the table."

Annise took ivory-colored ceramic mugs and plates out of the cupboard and set the bare wooden table. The knives had bone handles, but the spoons and forks were silver. She filled some wine glasses with red wine.

"Eduard, would you be so kind and tell Peter and Lukas we are about to eat?"

When the three men stepped into the cottage, Azelma screamed. "Oh I'm sorry," she said placing her hand on her chest, "But that little mouse running across the floor startled me. We simply have to get a cat."

"Yes, Mother, I would like that," Annise said and started pumping water at the sink for the men to wash their hands. They sat around the table while Azelma dished out the stew from a pot. After a brief prayer, they started eating.

"Good stew," said Lukas, somewhat surprised.

"So glad you like it. Eat as much as you want. Do you men have any plans for the evening?"

Peter looked at Lukas. "Since you are our guest, what would you like to do this evening?"

"Anything you suggest will be fine with me."

"Good, for I have made plans," said Peter with a big grin.

"You have?" said Azelma, looking surprised, for it was she who usually made the social plans.

"Yes, finish eating, and then we shall go somewhere. My surprise."

"Now I really am curious," said Azelma, eating faster.

Chapter 26

Supper was barely consumed when a carriage pulled by two chestnut horses stopped in front of the house. Peter went to the door and called to the driver,

"We'll be right with you!"

"What is going on?" Azelma asked while everyone else just gave Peter questioning looks.

"You complained the other day about having to plan all social events. Tonight everyone is doing something I planned. Get your wraps, everyone. We are going for a ride."

"Where to?" Annise asked, while rushing up the steps, to get a woolen shawl.

"You shall see," said her father a few seconds later, as she came down the stairs.

Eduard took her hand and led her into the carriage. She sat on the seat facing the back with Eduard besides her. Azelma sat in the seat facing the front with Peter and Lukas on either side of her.

When everyone had settled, Peter called to the driver to go. The man shook the reins, and the horses took off at a trot.

"Peter, where are we going? I have not even washed the dishes yet."

"They will wait. The *Sea Otter* sails in the morning, and there is someone we need to take leave of."

"Gabriel!" shouted Annise. "You should have told me we are going to see him. I made a sweater I want to give him."

"Is it this one?" Peter asked, reaching under his cloak.

"How did you know?"

"When you were first knitting, I asked you who it was for."

"And you remembered what I said," Annise said, surprised.

"My dear," Peter said with a grin, "I might be of the older generation, but I still have an intact mind."

"Then we are going to the ship?" observed Eduard.

"I expect everyone will be at the pubs tonight. We shall meet Gabriel at The Horse You Came In On."

"So that is where you have been riding off to," Azelma said, "testing all the horses for sale in Waterford. Have you found one you want to buy?"

"I'm really considering a gray Connemara pony. They are a wonderful breed—hardy, docile, and intelligent."

"I hope you will not keep him in the backyard, he would eat all the vegetables."

"No I would board him in a paddock near-by," said Peter. "How do you like Ireland so far, Marquis Lukas?"

"Please, just call me Lukas. You need not mention to anyone that I am a marquis. Let me just blend in, as all of you do."

"Lukas, in that outfit, you will never blend in," Eduard said. "But if you like, we can make a stop at a tailor shop. There is one as soon as we enter Passage East. He always has clothes for sale."

"Yes, let me stop and buy some local clothes," Lukas said, all excited.

Annise gave him an incredulous stare. "You are turning out to be a nice fellow, after all."

Lukas studied his shoes. "I am learning a lot on this journey."

The tailor was just locking the door of his shop when the coach stopped. "Please, sir," shouted Lukas jumping out of the carriage, "Could I make a quick purchase before you go home?"

The man unlocked and opened the door.

"Eduard, please come with me and help me shop."

Eduard smiled and rushed into the shop. A short time later, two laughing Irish men emerged. Lukas had bought clothes to match Eduard's—brown pants tying below the knees and white cable knit sweater. Lukas carried a bundle containing his old garments. Back in the carriage, Lukas asked the driver, "May I just keep my bundle of clothes in the carriage?"

"You may," the coachman said, "But no guarantee they will still be here when we come out."

"I shall hide them under the horse's feed," Lukas said with a shrug of the shoulders. "If someone steals them, so be it."

The carriage proceeded the short distance to The Horse You Came In On. They heard the music and laughter as they approached. Lukas laughed when he saw the name. "We are going to have fun tonight. Come, the first round is on me."

One table in the far corner had space after the American sailors slid closer together. A short time later they saw Gabriel walk in with Sami and Remi. Some energetic waving brought them to the table and everyone squeezed even closer. Two barmaids came over carrying mugs of frothy Guinness that Lukas bought for everyone at the table. He hardly had a sip, when a local girl urged him to dance with her. No sooner were they on the dance floor and the band played a fast jig. Lukas imitated the men dancing and surprised everyone how well he did it.

Back at the table, Eduard tapped him on the shoulder. "Lukas, I would like a word with you in private. Would you accompany me outside?"

Curious, Lukas followed Eduard. Once they were away from the building, he asked, "What is it you want to discuss?"

"Lukas, now tell me, is your father's name Hebert?"

"Yes, why?"

"And your grandmother is known as Lady Noelle de Castellane?"

"Yes, how do you know those names?"

"My mother was Lady de Castellane's maid about twenty-three years ago. Is the lady still with us?"

"Yes, she is. Lives with us in England. What are you saying?"

"I'll say it as simply as I can. You are my brother. Well, half-brother to be exact."

Lukas took a step back and stared at him with wide eyes and flared nostrils." Are you sure, or is it the ale talking?"

"If this is not what my mother told me, how would I know your grandmother's name? You can ask her if she remembers Rosalie Saulnier. Your father gave my mother a monthly pension until he left for England."

"You are my brother? I had a weird feeling about you from the beginning. When I came here, I was going to hate you. When I met you, I felt an immediate bond with you. I could not explain it, but now I know. Brother," he spread his arms wide, "Give me a hug."

"Thank you, I have no other siblings. I am glad to have a brother."

"Not only me, but you have two other brothers and one sister. We are all legitimate. As far as others like you, I have no idea." Tears filled Lukas's eyes and chocked his voice. "You are a decent and brave man, and I'm honored to call you my brother."

"Thank you. At first, I thought you were an insufferable snob, but underneath, you are a decent fellow yourself."

"I have all of you to thank for peeling away my haughty exterior. It was the way I was raised, and I knew no other way. It was not until I came here, that I really interacted with common people, and now I like it. Of course, these Irish people are not at all like the mobs of France."

"The mobs consist of once decent people who have been pushed to desperation with poverty and hunger. Those in power put all the resources into useless wars instead of seeing to the welfare of its citizens." Eduard saw Lukas's gaze wandering. "Enough of the political talk. Let's go back inside before we are missed too much."

"Good idea, I'm getting dry. Which one of us should announce to our friends that we are brothers?"

"How about we just…"

The two men walked into the pub with each having a hand on the other's shoulder. They spoke with the band which was between songs. The concertina player announced in a clear loud voice, "Quiet, everybody!"

After about a minute, everyone looked at the two men standing close to each other on the dance floor. Both of them called in unison, "We just want to inform everyone, that we are brothers."

People clapped and cheered. Annise rushed toward them and hugged first Eduard then Lukas.

"How exciting! When did you learn that? Tell us all about it."

"We can tell you on the carriage ride going home," Eduard said, placing his arm around her waist and walking back to the table.

"You two men are brothers?" Peter said, reaching out with both hands and wide eyes. "I had no idea you are a marquis."

"I'm no marquis, just the bastard son of one."

"As far as I'm concerned," Lukas said, "he is the noblest of all of my father's sons. I am honored to have him as my big brother."

"This is turning out be quite an evening," Azelma said. "We came here for a farewell party for Gabriel and our American friends, and now this. You two men look happy you found each other."

"Yes, all my life, I had only one relative, my mother. Now I have a brother too."

"And if I have any say," Lukas said with conviction, "you will have more relatives than that."

"That would be great. I see my friend Gabriel sitting so withdrawn. Come, brother, we need to talk with him."

When the two men approached Gabriel, he looked up with a forced grin. "My friend, this has been an exciting evening for you. I am glad to be here to share it with you."

"Brother, I want you to meet my best friend, Gabriel Sanson. Gabriel, this is Lukas de Castellane."

The two men shook hands. "A pleasure to meet a friend of my brother's. I hope to see more of you."

"This is our last time together, tomorrow I sail on the *Sea Otter*," Gabriel said, looking at Eduard with dull eyes. "I will miss you, my friend. I was hoping to see you get married, but that is not possible now. The captain says Sunday sails never fail."

"The wedding will not be for another six weeks. The Irish don't want anyone rushing into matrimony."

"That makes sense to me," Gabriel continued. "Not everyone has to prove their love like you did. If they did, there would be a lot fewer weddings." The music started again. "This is a catchy tune. I want to dance."

Gabriel hurried to the dance floor. Eduard reached for Annise and brought her to the floor, followed by Lukas and the count and countess. They all danced an Irish jig.

Chapter 27

It was well after midnight when the carriage with five exhausted people made its way to Waterford.

It was Eduard's and Lukas's intention to go into detail of their heritage, but they hardly started talking when they noticed everyone asleep.

"We might as well save the amusing story of our past for another day," Eduard said.

"I made reservations on the post coach for Monday," Lukas said, "and, Sunday, I need to attend mass. Father Pierre wants to perform an un-engagement ceremony."

"Yes, Annise mentioned it to me earlier. Don't you think you are a bit on the young side to get married?"

"I am eighteen."

"And to get married in England, you need your parent's consent until you are twenty-one. Doesn't that give you a message?"

"As it turns out, Annise will not be my wife, but my sister-in-law. That might even be better. I was just starting to enjoy my newly found manhood." Lukas cleared his throat and hesitated. "Tell me, brother, is she a lively steed?"

"That is a vulgar question and one a gentleman does not answer," Eduard said, waving a finger at Lukas. "We might dress like working people, but we still behave in a genteel manner."

"My deepest apology. I blame my indelicacy on strong drink."

Eduard was silent.

"Am I forgiven? Please say you forgive me."

"I forgive you, the subject is closed."

"Thank you. We are almost there." Lukas shook Peter's knee. "Time to wake up. You are home."

"Oh, so we are. I did have a little kip." *It is fun listening in when others think you don't hear them.* "Annise, Azelma, wake up. We are home."

"Already? That was a short ride," Azelma said, preparing to dismount the carriage. "Now don't forget to come to the ten o'clock mass tomorrow, I mean today."

"We shall be there," Eduard said, helping the ladies out of the carriage. "Goodnight."

"Goodnight," Annise said, giving Eduard her hand.

He kissed it. Without hesitation, she reached behind his neck and kissed him on the lips, before she followed her parents into the house.

cɔcɔ

The next morning, Lukas wanted to put on his regal clothes to go to mass. He remembered he had left them on the coach hidden under the hay. The coach, along with the horses was locked in the livery stable. He knocked on the door of Eduard's room. A sleepy Eduard opened the door with a puzzled look.

"Lukas, thank you for waking me. We have to hurry to church."

"I cannot go. I have no clothes to wear."

"What is wrong with the clothes you wore last night?"

"I cannot wear that to church."

"Of course you can. Instead of wearing my suit, I will wear what I wore last night, just to make you feel at ease. Now I have to rush to get ready. Meet you downstairs in just a few minutes."

"If you think it's appropriate, then I'll wear it. Those clothes are a lot more comfortable than what I traveled in."

"I'm going to convert you into a peasant yet." Eduard laughed and shut the door.

On the way to the cathedral, the two men caught up with the Brissons who were walking.

"Good morning, everyone," said Lukas with a bow and a sweep of the right arm. "I hope you had a good sleep?"

"Yes, thank you," said Azelma, giving both men a hug.

Annise hugged Eduard and just nodded at Lukas.

"We better hurry, or we shall be late for mass," Peter urged.

Service had just begun as they entered the sparsely occupied church. They sat near the middle, behind everyone else. An hour later, the service was over, and all the people slowly filed out. The five Frenchmen remained in their seats, and soon Father Pierre sought them out.

"Glad to see all of you here," he said in greeting. "We can begin the ceremony. Come up to the altar."

They followed the priest to the front of the church where one lit candle stood on the marble altar. He started chanting in Latin, that no one understood. Next, he handed Annise and Lukas an unlit candle.

"Now light your candle from the lit one." They both did. "Now both of you blow out the lit candle."

Lukas bent over to put his cheek next to Annise. Both took a deep breath and extinguished the small flame.

"Now you two young people are no longer engaged. Go your separate ways to find a spouse. God bless both of you."

Lukas shook the priest's hand. "Thank you, Father. If I was in England, I would invite you to the palace for dinner today."

"Father Pierre," said Azelma, "We have a big pot of stew at home. We would like to invite you to dinner at our humble cottage. I hope you don't mind eating beef stew again?" she asked, looking at everyone.

"Not at all," said Peter. "Your stew is always better on the second day. Come, Father, it is an honor to have you dine with us."

"It will be my pleasure, and it gives us the opportunity to get better acquainted. Give me a few minutes to get out of my chasuble." He went into a room behind the confessionals and soon reappeared in his black cassock and walking stick. "Lead on, my stomach is calling for stew."

As they left the church, Annise and Eduard held hands. She looked into his fawn brown eyes and smiled. "I just realized that, for a time, I was engaged to two men. Does that make me a bigamist?"

"No my love, that only applies to people who are married to more than one person." He gave her a quick kiss before they stepped out of the church.

The six Frenchmen spent the afternoon in the cottage and later in the garden, talking and drinking wine. Eventually, wedding plans came up in the conversation. Lukas just sat back and smiled.

ഗ∕ഗ

It was almost noon on Monday when Peter walked

with Lukas and Annise to the mail coach stop. Earlier that morning, Eduard bid his brother a teary farewell before he went to work at the newspaper. All three were dressed in Irish folk dress. The clothes Lukas came in were safely tucked in his leather bag.

As the coach approached, everyone could hear the mail guard blow a horn. The intimidating-looking guard sat next to the driver wearing a scarlet coat with blue lapels and gold braid fasteners on the front. On his head was a black top hat with gold braid. Armed with two pistols and a blunderbuss within reach, he discouraged any would-be highwaymen.

"Have a safe journey, young man," Peter said, shaking his hand.

"Thank you. And you, my dear Annise, have a wonderful wedding and a blessed life together."

He gave her a quick hug and boarded the coach. Seated in it was an old lady with a young girl. Both of them gave him friendly greetings with wide smiles.

Annise and her father were about to leave the mail drop when the postmaster called to them. "Miss Brisson, there is a package for you."

"I wager it is my fabric," she said reaching for the parcel. "Wonderful, now I can get ready for the wedding in earnest. Just think, *Pere*, in less than six weeks, I will be a married woman."

"We will miss having you in the house, but could not be more pleased with the son-in-law we're getting."

Chapter 28

It was a Wednesday morning in mid-August, and the sun awoke Annise. She jumped out of bed and rushed into the garden, still wearing her white nightgown.

Azelma, who had been up for hours, came out. "What are you doing out here in your nightgown?"

"*Mere,* today I am a bride, and according to Irish tradition, it is good luck if the sun shines on the bride. I just want to make sure the sun sees me, before clouds blow into the sky. We also have to listen for calls of birds. Please help me listen."

"I hear a sparrow."

"No, they don't count. Listen, Mama, do you hear that? There, from the woods. Yes, I am sure, it is a cuckoo."

"Yes, I hear it too. Now you are sure to have the blessings of good luck." Azelma hugged and kissed her daughter. "I have to take advantage and hug my little girl. In a few hours, you will be Mrs. Saulnier."

"I will always be your daughter. That will never change."

Several magpies flew by. "Look, magpies!" Annise shouted. "More signs of good luck."

"Wonderful, now you have all morning to do whatever you want to do. I need to go to O'Leary's and see to the festivities," Azelma said as they both walked into the kitchen.

"I would like to come with you and help."

"No, my dear, that is my job. I suggest you go to Eduard's cottage and make sure you have everything you need for your first night together. He is supposed to be at work this morning."

"The last time I checked, there was a large supply of honey wine, not to mention all the good things to eat. Where is *Pere* this morning?" Annise said, petting the half grown cat that had just lapped up a bowl of milk set on the floor.

"He is at O'Leary's. Are you ready for breakfast? We have some farina on the stove."

"Yes, I would like that," she said, picking up the orange and white cat they had named Goldie. "Do we still have some cherries?"

⸎

Annise arrived at the cottage Eduard was renting and had been living in for the past month. She found the door unlocked, stuck her head in, and called, "Is anyone here?"

From the second floor she heard a voice, "Yes, I'm here. Come on up."

"I was told you are at the *Chronicle*. Isn't it bad luck to see the bride before the wedding?"

"Only if she is wearing the wedding dress."

Annise ran up the steps into the bedroom. Eduard stood there with open arms and kissed her on the lips, long and deep.

"Oh, Eduard, I cannot wait to be with you night and day." They both flopped onto the wide bed and rolled around in an embrace. "My sweetheart, my soulmate, I can't wait for you to make me yours. Take me right now."

"I feel the same about you, but we have waited this long. You do not want to lose your virginity only hours before the vows are made before God and our friends and family. After today, we have the rest of our lives together."

He kissed her again with passion. Before they released the embrace, Annise looked out the window into the garden behind the house. "The apples are beginning to get red. I shall make apple cake and applesauce, and, hopefully, we can store some for winter. What time is it?"

"One o'clock," Eduard said, looking at his silver watch.

"I better get back. Some women are coming over at two to help me dress for the wedding."

"I know you will be the loveliest bride Waterford has ever seen. Farewell, my love, parting is such sweet sorrow."

"Shakespeare—Romeo and Juliet."

"You read that?" he said as they walked down the steps.

"Yes, in English too."

"Good for you." He embraced her once more and kissed her on the lips before she dashed away. He sighed as he watched her skip down the street. *I love her more than life. Please, Lord, keep her always safe and well.*

ণ৩৩৩

Peter waited at the post office for the mail coach to arrive. It seemed forever before he heard the horn announcing its arrival. Once the coach stopped, Lukas emerged and greeted Peter with a warm embrace. Next out of the coach was Marquis Hebert de Castellane. The two noblemen, both wearing dark suits of the middle class, shook hands before they broke into an embrace.

"Peter, so good to see you again. Lukas told me about the agony you and Azelma endured. And to think, the man who came to your rescue was my son. As a wedding present and reward for his brave actions, not only do I come, but—" The marquis reached into the coach and took the hand of a lady. "I have brought along his mother. Peter, meet Rosalie Saulnier."

An attractive forty-year-old woman, dressed in a long green cotton dress and a wide-brimmed natural straw hat, emerged from the coach. "It is a pleasure meeting you, Count de Brisson."

"The surprise and pleasure are all mine," Peter said, kissing her extended hand. "Just call me Peter. My wife will be so delighted to meet you. I cannot wait to see Eduard's face when he sees you. Are you going to stay in Ireland?"

"No, I will return to France. I am going to be married soon and will live with my husband in a small village north of Paris," she continued with sparkling eyes. "You cannot imagine my surprise when Marquis de Castellane contacted me. I knew about the wedding from Eduard, but for his father to invite me to travel with him—" Her voice choked and tears of joy filled her eyes.

"At first, my wife was thinking of coming too, but at the last minute had to cancel. She has a bad summer cold."

"I hope she feels better soon," Peter said. "Now I have arranged for you to meet Eduard in a private room in the cathedral a good hour before the ceremony. This will be a total surprise. We can go to O'Leary's first where I secured some rooms. Once there, you can meet my wife."

❧❧❧

Meanwhile, at the Brisson cottage, the women of the neighborhood were gathered in the spacious kitchen. They dressed the bride in a light-blue fine-linen gown with a form-fitting bodice and ornate silver hooks in the front. The white silk blouse had long sleeves edged with Irish lace. The skirt was split in the front, exposing the silk underskirt trimmed with Irish lace.

"You are a beautiful bride," said one girl named Colleen, with the other half dozen women agreeing full-heartedly. "Now Kathy will do your hair."

Kathy brought the long hair from the front and top of the head and made an elaborate Celtic knot on the back of the head. Next, she took some of Annise's straight, blonde hair, made two thin braids, and connected them in the back. Meanwhile, a brass rod with a wooden handle was heating on the stove.

"What are you going to do with that?" Annise asked, alarmed, as Kathy approached her waist length hair.

"Don't worry." She showed how well it curled hair on another neighbor. "See? We have a curl, and it did not burn the hair."

In a short time, the bride had large curls in her long hair.

"Now, for the final touch," said Colleen, "We put the bridal wreath on your head."

She took a ring of flowers consisting of blue lavender and white daisies and placed it on Annise's head. Next, she handed her a bouquet of the same flowers. Two lace ribbons dangled out of the bouquet, on the ends of which were two small crystal horseshoes. A lace edged linen handkerchief was used to tie the flowers together.

Annise studied herself in the mirror and was pleased. "Thank you ladies for all your help. Now I have to wait for my parents to come with the bridal carriage. I hope it is soon."

❧❧❧

While the bride was getting dressed, the groom was in the same process in his cottage. Peter was the only other person present. Both men wore black suits. Eduard's lapel was decorated with one daisy and some lavender.

"This should be the happiest day of my life, but I also feel sad," said Eduard.

"Why are you sad?"

"I think of my mother, back in Paris by herself." Eduard sniffed and wiped his nose. "She was a good mother, and I do miss her. And I have never met my father. It was not until my birthday this year my mother told me who he is."

"I'm surprised she waited until you are twenty-two."

"She said it was because I was born on the twenty-second of February. She believes there is something special about the number two in my life. What it is, I have not figured out." He looked in the mirror and combed his short curly hair. "It was great meeting my brother, and I wish he could be here today, but I understand. It is a long trip from England."

"I hope Annise's mother and I will be considered your family in a few hours."

"I have done that for a long time already."

The two men hugged.

"Come, it is time to go to church and make our relationship official. I will drop you off, then get Azelma and pick up the bride."

"What will I do by myself in church the whole time?"

"Father Pierre wants to talk with you."

"Father Pierre and I are just about talked out by now," Eduard said with a sigh.

Chapter 29

The two men sat in silence in the carriage pulled by two white horses. Eduard's eyes were downcast as he emerged from the carriage and walked up the few steps toward the front door of the cathedral. A tall man stood near the door. Eduard proceeded to pass him when the man spoke.

"What is wrong, brother, don't you even greet me?"

"Lukas, my dear Lukas, you came. How wonderful."

The two men hugged.

"What a surprise," Eduard continued. "I am so glad you came. You make my day complete."

"Come inside, there is someone else who came."

"Who, my friend Gabriel?"

"No, come and see."

The two men entered a small side room and the first person Eduard noticed was a lady. "Mother, you have come." He rushed to embrace her. "How wonderful."

"Yes, my son, and there is someone I want you to meet." She motioned toward the tall man a few feet away. "Eduard, meet Marquis Hebert de Castellane, your father."

Eduard's knees went weak. He steadied himself on the back of a chair and sat down. For a good minute, he stared open-mouthed at the forty-year-old man. Finally, he whispered, "Father, is it really you?"

The marquis walked over to Eduard and extended his hands. Eduard took them and stood up, still speechless.

"I am proud to call you my son. I have heard of your bravery and what you have done for my two friends, the Brissons. I hope we will be able to entertain you and your bride in our place in England before too long. You have three more siblings who could not come, but are eager to meet you."

"My mother and father and I in the same room. This is something I never believed would ever happen." Eduard hugged the marquis and extended his arm toward his mother. She entered the embrace and tears rolled down her face. "And you, my brother. It is because of you we are now together." Eduard took a handkerchief out of his pocket and dried his mother's tears. "I hear the organ playing. Are you ready to go into the church and watch me get married?"

"It cannot be a moment too soon," Rosalie said. "I want to see what an Irish wedding looks like."

"We are also including French traditions," Eduard explained. "One of them is, and I never thought I would be able to do it, I will proudly walk you, *Mere*, down the aisle and seat you in the front row." Looking at the marquis and Lukas, he said, "I hope both of you will sit in the front row too."

"I would be honored if you call me Father or *Pere*."

"Thank you," Eduard said, biting his lips. "I hear the bells. The bride must be arriving."

Hebert and Lukas walked down the long aisle and took their place in the first row. Next, Eduard walked with his mother on his arm. Both were beaming. He seated her next to the two men. At the same time, Father Pierre stepped out from behind the altar and faced the half-filled church. He smiled at the groom and motioned for him to stand next to him.

The organ started playing "Greensleeves." Everyone stood up and looked toward the back of the church. Peter and Azelma walked down the aisle, with Annise between them. Azelma's dress was the same style, only darker and not as ornate. All three glowed with joy.

When they reached the altar, Peter placed his daughter's hand into Eduard's and sat down with his wife. The organ was still playing. Annise looked at Rosalie and the marquises and gave them a happy smile.

Within the hour, the ceremony was concluded, and

the happy couple went to the vestibule and waited for everyone to wish them well. The first one to kiss the bride was her father-in-law. Another good omen, because it was a man. Then Rosalie gave her a warm hug and kiss.

With a choking voice, Annise said, "You cannot imagine how happy I am you are here. Eduard has spoken of you often. Please stand next to your son and greet the guests."

Rosalie felt a lump in her throat and could not speak. All she managed was to smile with teary eyes as she took her place in the receiving line. The marquis also greeted the other two hundred or so guests.

When just about everyone had expressed their congratulations, a band materialized and led the wedding party to O'Leary's. The celebration went well into the next day.

It was after midnight, and the bride and groom were able to slip away unnoticed and make their way to his cottage.

"Do we dare make love?" Annise asked before they went upstairs.

"We better try to get some sleep," Eduard said with shaky laughter. "The bed might be rigged to make noise or fall down if anything exciting goes on. Just think, we have the rest of our lives to sleep together."

"This has been the most exciting and wonderful day of my life," Annise said, giving him a big kiss. "It is the first of many wonderful days and years to come."

"That it is, my love, with God's help, that it is."

Hand in hand they walked up the steps and into the bedroom.

THE END

About the Author

When Ellynore Seybold was just a kid, she knew she wanted to be a writer. Her first book, The Wooden Mistress, was published in 1994. Then in 2012, Seybold was diagnosed with cancer. She thought, if it was time to die, okay. After all, her husband was waiting on the other side. Then a miracle happened, and the tumor turned benign. Seybold saw this as a message from God that she had better do something creative with the rest of her life. And she began to write in earnest.